Stephanie Olds

THE UNSEEN LEDGER: Without Announcement

The Unseen Ledger: Without Announcement
by Stephanie Olds

Printed in the United States of America
December 2025
ISBN: 978-1968178345

Ink and Revival Publishing
Virginia, USA

We live in a world that often rewards appearances over substance and volume over truth. In spaces driven by attention and visibility, it's easy to wonder whether integrity still counts when it isn't being applauded.

I believe it does.

This story is not about influence, trends, or being seen. It is about what forms quietly when no one is looking—the habits we keep, the care we show, and the honesty we choose even when cutting corners would be easier. It asks whether character still leaves a trace, and whether sincerity carries weight in a world obsessed with performance.

I believe there is an unseen order to things. That what is done in secret matters. That truth accumulates, even slowly. God is not distracted by spectacle, nor misled by imitation. He sees clearly, weighs honestly, and honors what is real.

Living with integrity is not fast and it is rarely rewarded immediately. But it is not wasted. Authenticity is not weakness; it is faith in motion.

This book is an invitation to trust that what you cultivate—quietly, faithfully, honestly—still matters.

With intention,

Table of Contents

PART I

ONE: The Magenta Garden 1

TWO: Thick Glasses, Thin Air 11

THREE: Not for the Feed 23

FOUR: The Elephant Drawer 41

FIVE: A Bouquet for Ms. Dollard 57

PART II

SIX: The Day It Arrived 75

SEVEN: Roots and Wings 95

EIGHT: When Praise Feels Like Theft 107

NINE: The Ceremony 117

TEN: Still, They Knew 133

PART III

ELEVEN: The Video That Missed the Point 145

TWELVE: The Weight of Being Seen 155

THIRTEEN: The Offer That Made Sense 167

FOURTEEN: The Girl Who Said Yes 183

FIFTEEN: Without Announcement 197

SIXTEEN: Legacy Has a Voice 211

PART I

SEEDS

CHAPTER ONE

The Magenta Garden

Some things grow best where no one is looking.

By the time the sun eased its way over the row of weathered brick houses on Birchwood Lane, Mira's hands were already buried in the morning soil. She knelt in the narrow patch of backyard her mother affectionately called *The Miracle*—not because anything extraordinary happened there, but because it was the only part of their modest rental home that grew with stubborn, dependable life. Everything else in the yard was unpredictable: patchy grass, dull hedges, one scrawny tree that refused to bloom on time. But Mira's garden thrived with quiet determination, just like she did.

Her hoodie hung from her narrow shoulders, sleeves smudged with soil, and her long ponytail kept sliding forward over her shoulder no matter how many times she tucked it back. Her thick glasses repeatedly slipped down her nose, and she pushed them up with the back of her wrist, leaving faint streaks of dirt across the lenses. Still, she worked with calm precision, inspecting each tulip bud like she expected it to whisper back.

"Okay, y'all," she murmured to the row of tulips in front of her, "today is the day you stop playing with me."

The tulips didn't answer—of course they didn't—but in the pale morning light, their tight green buds looked a little less stubborn, as if they might finally consider blooming. She had planted them in a crescent around an old cinderblock that once sat forgotten near the fence line. It had been ugly—gray, chipped, uninspired. Last summer she'd painted it magenta and stenciled white butterflies along its top. Now sun-faded around the edges, the block still glowed from the dirt like a secret.

Magenta tulips around a magenta stone.
"Match your energy," she'd instructed them in the fall, and she meant it.

Mira pressed her thumb gently into the soil around one tulip stem, testing the moisture. Not too wet. Not too dry. Perfect.

Behind her, the screen door creaked open and clapped shut.

"Mira, baby," her mother called from the steps, voice warm and still wrapped in sleep. "You out here talking to those flowers again?"

"Talking is a strong word," Mira said without turning around. "I'm just… encouraging."

Delilah laughed, soft and amused. "Well, encourage yourself back inside in ten minutes. Bus comes early on Mondays."

"Okay!"

Mira listened as her mother walked back inside—heard the faint clatter of cabinets, the hum of the refrigerator, and gospel music playing through a little static. Their family moved at a slightly slower speed than the rest of the world. Older appliances, older car, older everything. But their home held together. Mostly.

A jingling bell sounded from behind her. Mira turned just as Professor Butterbean—their orange-and-white foster-fail cat—strode onto the steps with the confidence of a landlord inspecting his property. He had been meant to stay temporarily, but from the first night he curled up on Mira's chest and refused to leave, it was clear the arrangement was permanent.

He pressed his forehead to her elbow, then sat down beside her with a regal air, tail wrapped neatly around his paws.

"Good morning, Professor," Mira said, scratching behind his ear. He leaned into her touch with the kind of loyalty he gave no one else—not even Delilah.

A soft yellow butterfly drifted lazily over the fence and hovered above the magenta stone. Professor

Butterbean tracked it with serious suspicion but didn't move. Mira watched the butterfly's uncertain flutter, fascinated. Butterflies always acted like they hadn't realized their bodies were designed for flight.

"Good morning," she whispered to it.

Her phone buzzed in her hoodie pocket, but she finished circling mulch around a tulip before checking it. A row of notifications lit her screen:

New post from: @KrysKrysKool
New post from: @TrendLabOfficial
New DM from: Jaya 🦋

The butterfly emoji had followed Jaya's name for years—ever since ten-year-old Mira declared butterflies and elephants were her "spirit animals."

Jaya 🦋:
u up already?? 👀

Jaya 🦋:
tell me u didn't set an alarm to go whisper to the lettuce again

Mira smirked.

Mira:
they're tulips
& i don't whisper
i deliver motivational speeches

Three dots. Disappeared. Returned.

Jaya 🦋:
LMAOOO
ok Dr. Plant
check TT when u come in
NEED u 2 see this trend, it's so dumb 💀

Mira slipped her phone back into her pocket. TikTok could wait. The garden couldn't.

A siren wailed faintly three streets over. A car horn honked twice. The world was waking up in layers. Mira leaned closer to the tulip bed, searching for any hint of color along the bud seams.

Still green. Still secret.

"You're allowed to be late," she murmured. "It's not a race."

If someone had walked past just then, they would have seen a tall, lanky Black girl in an oversized gray hoodie, kneeling barefoot in the dirt, her glasses fogged at the edges and smudged from soil. Awkward, maybe. Out of place in the way tenderhearted kids often are. But the way she handled the earth—with care, reverence, patience—made the entire yard feel different.

The garden wasn't big, but to Mira, it was a mapped universe. One corner held herbs—basil, mint, rosemary—plants she used in meals or rubbed between her fingers just for the scent. Another corner held vegetables: collards growing unevenly but faithfully, a tomato plant supported by a crooked cage, peppers still deciding their fate.

Closest to the house were her experiments: seeds from grocery-store bell peppers, lemon pits nestled in jars, a discarded succulent she refused to let die. To an outsider, the area looked chaotic. To Mira, every sprout was a quiet yes from the earth.

She brushed a leaf. "You're doing great," she told them all.

A second butterfly appeared—this one blue—and landed on a narrow stem that bent but didn't break. Mira smiled at its confidence.

The screen door banged open again.

"Seven minutes!" Delilah called. "Shoes, teeth, backpack—move it, Miss Farmer!"

"I'm coming!"

Mira set the watering can aside, wiped her hands on her leggings, and looked over her garden one final time—the magenta stone, the stubborn buds, the promise that something beautiful was on its way.

"Grow slow," she whispered. "Grow strong."

Then she jogged toward the house, ponytail swinging, lanky legs half a step faster than her balance.

Professor Butterbean trotted after her but stopped just inside the threshold, settling into a loaf shape to guard the entry.

Inside, warmth gathered in the kitchen like a second presence. Toast popped. Eggs sizzled in the pan. Gospel music hummed through the radio. Delilah stood at the stove with her purple headscarf tied neatly, work badge clipped to her scrub top, shoulders holding both fatigue and resilience.

Her mother had a presence—not loud, but solid. She filled a room without trying, her spirit taking up more space than her body ever did.

"You wash?" Delilah asked without turning.

"I'm literally on my way," Mira said, heading for the sink.

She scrubbed her hands with lemon soap, dried them with the worn blue towel, and sat at the table as her mother slid a warm plate in front of her.

"Eat," Delilah said. "I don't want a call from the school nurse again about somebody fainting in homeroom."

"That was once."

"That was twice," Delilah corrected.

Professor Butterbean brushed against Mira's leg, purring like a polite engine. Delilah narrowed her eyes. "See? He doesn't even acknowledge me."

"He loves you," Mira said.

"He tolerates me," Delilah shot back. "He adores you. If he had thumbs, he'd probably braid your hair for you."

Mira grinned. "He likes my cooking better."

"That is factual." Delilah smirked. "Speaking of—did you watch that video I sent you last night? The little girl with the cookie business?"

"Yes."

"She's ten and already has investors," Delilah said, shaking her head. "Makes you think."

Mira chewed slowly, absorbing the meaning beneath her mother's tone. Some kids seemed to stumble into opportunity like it waited specifically for them.

Others—kids like her—grew opportunities like plants: slowly, quietly, with no guaranteed bloom.

Delilah capped her travel mug. The lid clicked softly. Her expression softened.

"Baby… you don't have to be famous to have a purpose. Or loud. Or the center of anything. But I want you to have choices. Options. That's why I nudge you sometimes."

"I know," Mira said. And she did. Deeply.

"Good. Now hurry up. That bus will not wait for your philosophical plant speeches."

Mira scarfed down the last bite of eggs, rinsed her plate, grabbed her backpack, and bent to kiss Professor Butterbean's head. He pretended not to like it, but his tail curled in approval.

Outside, the morning warmed slightly. A neighbor dragged a trash can. A stereo blared music too early for anyone reasonable but somehow fitting for their street.

Delilah locked the door and walked Mira to the edge of the porch.

"Text me when you get there."

"I will."

Delilah brushed a thumb across her daughter's cheek. "You're growing into yourself," she said softly. "I see it. Don't rush."

Mira nodded, shoulders tightening the way they always did when compliments came too close.

She walked toward the bus stop, then glanced back. She couldn't see the garden from the street, but she felt it—quiet, patient, storing strength beneath the surface.

Behind the house, one tulip bud loosened just enough to reveal a sliver of magenta.

No one saw it.

The day was unfolding exactly as it should.

CHAPTER TWO

Thick Glasses, Thin Air

Attention is loud. Influence is quiet.

The hallway at Northside Middle School had a sound all its own — a strange mix of chatter, slamming metal doors, sneaker squeaks, and the perpetual hum of the overhead lights that buzzed like tired bees. Mira walked through it with the kind of practiced caution she usually reserved for carrying a tray of muffins across the kitchen. Not fearful, just… aware. Tall girls with long limbs had to be mindful of their surroundings, especially in crowded hallways designed for seventh graders who hadn't yet discovered personal space.

Her backpack thumped lightly against her shoulder blades as she moved along the left side of the hall, close to the lockers. The building smelled faintly of cleaning spray, paper, and the biscuits they served every morning in the cafeteria. She'd eaten at home, but she didn't mind the smell. It made the day feel warmer.

A couple of kids sat on the floor filming themselves reenacting some TikTok joke Mira didn't recognize. Another group blocked the hallway entirely, trying to capture a slow-motion walk-out moment with synchronized hair flips. Mira stepped around them, careful not to walk through the center of the shot. The last time she did that, they made her the villain of a twenty-second clip that got passed around until people forgot the original video but remembered that "some tall girl" had ruined the lighting.

She didn't mind being ignored. She preferred it. But she hated causing trouble, even accidentally.

A voice cut through the noise. "MIIIRAAAA!"

She turned just in time to see Jaya squeezing between two boys twice her size, waving with enough enthusiasm to power a wind turbine. Jaya always looked a little like someone had dared her to create her own weather. Today, her hair was braided into two thick ropes wrapped with navy-blue ribbon, and she wore an orange hoodie with hand-drawn stars on the sleeves.

"You left me on read," Jaya said when she reached her. "Rude. Abandoning me in my time of entertainment crisis."

"I wasn't abandoning," Mira said, adjusting her glasses. "I was busy. The tulips needed attention."

"The tulips," Jaya repeated, deadpan. "Your plants are draining your social battery."

"They don't ask me to watch videos at six-fifteen in the morning."

"Well," Jaya said, linking their arms as they walked, "I'm asking you now."

They turned down the main hallway that led to their homeroom. Mira could feel the familiar morning stiffness in her legs, that awkward too-long feeling she still hadn't grown into. Some days she wished she were a little shorter, or at least less noticeable. But on days like this, when she had Jaya beside her — with her bright voice and confident stride — being tall didn't matter as much.

Jaya unlocked her phone and held it out. "Okay, prepare yourself. The 'Be Kind, Go Viral' trend is officially worse than the one from last month where everyone pretended to faint in public."

"I hated that one," Mira said. "Too many people hit the tile floor without thinking it through."

"Right? But this one… this one might be worse." Jaya tapped the screen. A video began playing — soft piano music, warm filters, and a girl in their grade speaking tearfully into the camera.

"I just want to do something meaningful," the girl said dramatically. "So today, I bought a sandwich for someone who needed it. Please… be kind."

The comments were full of heart emojis and "you're an angel" messages.

Mira tilted her head. "Did she need to record it?"

"That's the whole thing!" Jaya said. "The ORIGINAL video — the one some girl in Nebraska made — wasn't even a trend. She just filmed herself helping her elderly neighbor mow the lawn because he hurt his back. It was sweet. And now—" she gestured to the screen, "—everyone is recreating it with fake tears and inspirational quotes."

Mira handed the phone back, eyebrows raised. "People always copy things. That's what the internet does."

"Yeah, but this time they're copying kindness," Jaya said. "It feels… cheap."

Mira didn't say anything. She just tucked a loose piece of hair back into her ponytail and continued walking. She didn't like when people performed goodness. It wasn't something she could articulate exactly, but it made her feel like she had swallowed something too sweet too fast.

As they reached their classroom door, a boy with a ring light clipped to his backpack stepped in front of them.

"Have you seen my version yet?" he asked proudly. "Uploaded it this morning. I did slow motion, added a grain filter, and used the trending audio. It's gonna hit half a million, easy."

"That's great," Jaya said, smiling in a way that was polite but clearly forced.

"Make sure you share it," he added before darting off to film himself opening the classroom door as though he were entering a concert stage.

Mira exhaled slowly as they took their seats. "He's going to hurt himself trying to keep up with that."

"Absolutely," Jaya said. "But he'll do it with perfect lighting."

Mrs. Clay entered the room carrying a stack of fliers and a cup of iced coffee that clinked with melting cubes. "Good morning, everyone," she said, already sounding tired. "We've got a few announcements today. First, the Tether Emerging Creators Scholarship."

A low murmur spread across the room. Everyone knew the scholarship was a big deal — five thousand dollars, mentorship opportunities, public recognition. It was the kind of thing people applied to with carefully edited videos, elaborate portfolios, and rehearsed speeches.

Mira sat up straighter, even though she didn't intend to apply.

"The district mentioned," Mrs. Clay continued, "that there may be a new selection process this year."

"New how?" someone asked.

Mrs. Clay shrugged. "They didn't specify. But the recipient will be announced Friday."

That was sooner than expected. Several students exchanged excited or panicked looks. One girl immediately began whispering to her friend about re-editing her audition tape. A boy pulled out a sketchbook, flipping through it anxiously.

Jaya nudged Mira. "You should go for it."

"I don't have anything to submit," Mira whispered back.

"You cook. You bake. You garden. You read more books than the library owns. That counts."

"But it's not the kind of creating they mean," Mira replied, looking down at her notebook.

She didn't want to disappoint Jaya, but Mira knew herself. She didn't make content — she made things. Meals that comforted people. Little gardens that healed hurt soil. Quiet creations that mattered privately. Putting all that on display felt wrong, like showing strangers the inside of a diary.

The bell rang, and the hallway erupted again. Mira gathered her books and followed the crowd out. Her glasses fogged slightly as the temperature shifted, and she wiped them with the sleeve of her hoodie.

The hallway was more chaotic than before. A group of kids had blocked one end of the corridor and were directing each other in "kindness poses" for their videos. One girl kept re-tying her ponytail because she didn't like how it swayed in the clip.

"Hold the sandwich higher," someone instructed. "And tilt your chin. People look more generous from that angle."

Mira paused only long enough to take in the absurdity before continuing down the opposite direction. She didn't feel angry. She didn't even feel superior. She simply felt… tired. Tired of seeing things meant to be genuine get swallowed by performance.

There was a difference between doing something good and staging yourself doing something good. She didn't know why that mattered so much to her, but it always had.

She rounded the corner and nearly ran into a group of eighth graders. They parted just enough for her to slip through, murmuring apologies as she went. She didn't notice anything unusual, no shift in the air, no invisible force taking note of her actions.

All she noticed was that someone had spilled juice near the lockers again, leaving a sticky patch that would catch shoes all day.

Mira stepped around it carefully.
There was nothing symbolic about it. Just sticky floors and a busy Monday.

Her life, for now, was ordinary.

And that was enough.

She'd almost made it to the stairwell when she heard a sharp intake of breath behind her, followed by the scrape of metal against tile.

"—sorry, sorry—"

Mira turned.

A girl stood a few lockers back, frozen in place, one hand gripping the bar of a rolling backpack that had caught awkwardly against the sticky patch of floor. The wheels were angled wrong, refusing to move forward or back. The girl's shoulders were tense, her face flushed with the effort of not panicking in a public place.

Mira recognized her vaguely — same grade, maybe a class or two apart. She wore noise-canceling headphones, thick and padded, pushed slightly off one ear. One of her shoes was scuffed at the toe, the laces unevenly tied.

"Hold on," Mira said, already stepping closer.

The girl startled slightly, then nodded. "It gets… stuck sometimes."

"I see," Mira said, kneeling without thinking.

She pressed her palm against the floor, testing it the way she tested soil. Sticky. Not wet, just tacky enough to grab rubber. Mira angled the wheels, lifted slightly, then guided the backpack around the patch with slow, deliberate movements.

"There," she said. "Try now."

The girl rolled the backpack forward. It moved smoothly. Her shoulders dropped an inch.

"Thank you," she said, quiet but precise. "Most people just… walk around."

"Well," Mira said, standing and wiping her hand on her leggings, "that doesn't un-stick anything."

The girl smiled at that — a small smile, but real. She adjusted her headphones, then hesitated, as if deciding whether to say more.

"I'm Alina," she said. "I like your glasses."

"Thanks," Mira said. "I'm Mira."

Alina nodded once, like she was filing the information carefully. "You always take the left side of the hall. Fewer people bump you."

Mira blinked. "You noticed that?"

Alina shrugged. "I notice patterns. Crowds are loud even when they don't sound like it."

Mira felt something settle in her chest. Recognition, maybe. Not excitement. Just understanding.

"I like your backpack," Mira said. "It looks sturdy."

"It is. My dad reinforced the bottom because the wheels kept breaking. I carry… a lot."

"Books?"

"Mostly." Alina paused. "And some things I make."

"Like what?"

Alina glanced toward the stairwell, then back. "Crochet. Mostly. Hats. Animals. I sell a few online. Not many."

"That's cool," Mira said, meaning it.

They stood there for a second longer than necessary, neither rushed, neither awkward. Just present.

A shout echoed from farther down the hall — someone laughing too loudly, a chorus of phones being lifted at once.

Alina slipped her headphones fully back on. "I should go before it gets louder."

"Yeah," Mira said. "Me too."

They walked together toward the stairs, not close enough to touch but aligned in pace. At the doorway, Alina stopped.

"Your helping," she said, halting. "You didn't film it."

Mira frowned slightly. "Why would I?"

Alina's mouth twitched. "Just checking."

Then she disappeared down the stairwell, one hand trailing along the railing.

Mira stood there for a moment, feeling the hallway surge around her again as if nothing had happened. Students continued past. Voices bounced. Shoes stuck briefly to the floor and peeled away.

No one had noticed the small fix.
No one had commented.
No one had filmed.

She adjusted her glasses and kept walking.

Later, in science class, Mira caught sight of Alina again through the glass-paneled lab door. She sat at the edge of a shared table while two other students argued loudly about whose turn it was to record their experiment. Alina worked silently, hands steady as she measured liquid into a beaker, movements precise and careful.

At lunch, Mira spotted her in the corner nearest the windows, headphones on, sketching small figures into a notebook while her food sat untouched for a few minutes too long.

There was a hum to the day — not spiritual, not strange — just the sense that people were moving through it at wildly different volumes.

When the final bell rang, Mira packed her things and headed out, the encounter lingering not as a *moment* but as a *weight* — the kind that didn't press down, only reminded you something mattered.

CHAPTER THREE

Not for the Feed

What spreads fastest is not always what lasts.

By the time the bus dropped her off that afternoon, Mira's head felt full of other people's voices. Snippets of conversations, the echo of fake sobbing from the "Be Kind, Go Viral" videos some kids had replayed at lunch, the way everyone's sentences seemed to end in, "Don't forget to like and subscribe."

The minute she stepped through the front door, the house felt mercifully quieter. The TV was off. The radio played low in another room. The air carried the faint smell of coffee and whatever her mother had reheated for lunch between shifts.

"Hey, baby," Delilah called from the hallway. "Good day?"

"It was a day," Mira said, dropping her backpack onto its usual spot by the chair.

"That bad, huh?"

"Just loud."

Delilah popped her head around the doorway, keys in one hand, phone in the other, her scrubs already on. "I have to head back in a few. Left some chicken in the fridge for you to experiment on. Don't burn my house down."

"I make no promises," Mira said.

Delilah gave her a look that said she knew better. "Text me if you go anywhere. Love you."

"Love you."

The door shut behind her mother with a soft click. Silence settled more fully. Professor Butterbean emerged from the bedroom like he'd been waiting for the exact moment the house became theirs again. He stretched, yawned without apology, then trotted over to bump his head against Mira's shin.

"You survived another day without me," Mira said. "Barely."

He meowed in fragile protest, as if the hours had been unbearable.

She scratched under his chin. "Want to help me cook?"

He followed her as she walked into the kitchen, his bell jingling lightly with each step.

The kitchen looked tired, but it was hers. The laminate counters were scratched and the oven door squeaked when you opened it too fast, but Mira knew where every pan lived, which burner ran too hot, how long the light above the stove flickered before finally committing. She pulled open the fridge and surveyed the contents: chicken thighs, half a bag of carrots, a sad-looking onion, some celery starting to limp, a wedge of lemon, a carton of broth. There was rice in the pantry. She could work with that.

"Chicken and rice?" she asked the cat, as if he had any culinary say.

He jumped onto the chair by the table and watched her with narrowed eyes, tail curled neatly around his paws, as if grading her technique.

"That's a yes," she decided.

Professor Butterbean leapt onto the counter before she could stop him, tail flicking in anticipation. Mira shook her head, smiling as she pulled ingredients from the fridge.

She didn't think about Alina as she chopped carrots. She didn't think about likes or trends or videos.

She thought about how some things worked better when handled gently.

How not everything needed an audience.

How being useful didn't always look impressive.

When she set her phone up against the sugar canister, it wasn't because she wanted to share something special.

It was simply because she was already doing something that felt worth remembering.

She tied on the apron her aunt had given her last Christmas—white cotton with little green leaves printed along the hem—and rolled up her hoodie sleeves. The rhythm came back quickly: rinse, pat dry, season, chop. The board thunked softly as the knife moved through carrots and celery. The onion made her eyes water, but she didn't mind. It felt like her body's way of acknowledging the work.

After a few minutes, she propped her phone up against the sugar canister, angling it toward the cutting board. The camera showed a slightly crooked view of her hands and the ingredients. No ring light. No overhead tripod. Just the counter, the food, and whatever light the window bothered to give them.

She hit record.

"Okay," she murmured, mostly to herself but technically to whoever might watch later. "Chicken and rice… soothing edition."

She didn't talk much while she cooked. It wasn't a show. She narrated just enough so that if Jaya asked for the recipe, she wouldn't have to type it out step by step. A little salt here. A sprinkling of thyme. A squeeze of lemon. She showed how to brown the chicken skin so it crisped rather than steamed. The phone caught the hiss of contact as the pieces hit the hot pan.

Professor Butterbean's head followed each movement like he was watching a very serious documentary.

When everything was assembled in the pot—chicken nestled into rice and vegetables, broth poured over top—Mira set a lid on it and turned the heat down low. She stopped the recording and wiped her hands on a dish towel before picking up the phone.

The video was a little shaky. The angle was slightly off. The audio captured the hum of the refrigerator in the background. But when she watched it, she felt… calm. This looked like what cooking really felt like in their house. No music. No voice-over. Just hands, food, and care.

She trimmed the start and end, added the text: **Simple Chicken & Rice for Tired Days**, and hovered over the sound options for a moment. She skipped the trending audios. They didn't match the mood. Instead, she turned the sound down just enough so the sizzling wasn't too harsh.

Her follower count wasn't impressive. A few family members, some girls from school, a handful of strangers who had stumbled across her earlier baking experiments and stayed. She wasn't trying to grow it. The feed felt more like a diary than a stage.

She hit post anyway.

For a moment, she imagined the video slipping into the millions of other clips floating around online, just one more tiny square in an endless stack. Then she put the phone face-down on the table and focused on the smell rising from the pot. The broth thickened, rice puffing up, chicken skin turning a deep golden brown. Professor Butterbean crept closer, nose twitching.

"You're not getting any of this," she told him. "Vet said no more people food."

He flicked his tail in outraged disbelief.

By the time the rice was done, the kitchen was full of steam and the kind of smell that made you feel hugged. Mira scooped some into a bowl, let it cool, and carried it to the table, setting a glass of water beside it. She didn't photograph the finished dish.

That part felt too intimate. This bowl was for her, not for anyone watching through a screen.

She had eaten half of it before she remembered her phone. When she checked, the video had a modest trickle of notifications—six likes, two comments.

auntie_dee:
this is real food 🤍 save me a plate next time

ms_dollard_nextdoor:
Looks delicious, sweetheart. Smells like it too 👀

Mira smiled. She hadn't realized Ms. Dollard even had an account. She pictured the older woman sitting on her sagging couch with her tablet, watching young people cook meals that were sometimes more art project than dinner.

She replied to both, then set the phone aside again. That felt like enough.

The next morning, the hallway felt slightly louder than usual. Mira chalked it up to midweek restlessness until she heard her name.

"Yo, Mira!" a boy called from behind her. "You see Levi's new video? It's insane."

She turned as a cluster of students crowded around someone holding up a phone. It took her a second to realize the someone was Levi—the ring-light boy from the kindness trend, his hair brushed into a style that didn't quite obey him.

"What's he doing now?" Jaya asked, sliding in beside Mira.

"Cooking," the boy who'd called out said. "Like, chef-level stuff. Look at this."

They leaned in just enough to see the screen without committing to the huddle.

Levi's video was slick. The lighting was bright and even. The angles shifted rapidly—close-up on his hands, overhead shot of the pot, quick cuts synced to a trending audio track. The text across the screen read: **Comfort Chicken & Rice You'll Want Every Week**. He twirled a wooden spoon dramatically at the camera between steps.

Mira's brain took a moment to catch up. The ingredients were familiar. Chicken thighs. Carrots. Celery. Onion. Lemon. Rice. He seasoned them almost exactly the way she had. The knife moved through the vegetables in the same order. The camera paused on the same moment the broth poured in, catching the swirl of steam.

Her chest tightened.

Jaya's eyes narrowed. "Wait," she said slowly. "Didn't you—"

"Yeah," Mira said quietly.

The video cut to a shot of Levi lifting the lid, steam billowing. The music swelled. He plated the food into a pristine white bowl, sprinkling something green over the top that he didn't bother to identify. The final frame showed the bowl on a wooden board, shot from above, his hand entering the frame to grab the fork.

The like count ticked upward even as they watched. Hundreds. Then a thousand. The comments poured in so fast the screen blurred.

omg this is comfort in a bowl
posting this to my story brb
"chef Levi" has entered the chat
drop the full recipe king

"He posted that late last night," the boy said. "It's blowing up. Could hit For You Page for real."

"It already did," another student said. "I've seen like four people share it."

Jaya glanced at Mira, then at the video again. "This looks… familiar," she said, louder this time.

"Cooking videos all look the same," someone else shrugged. "I mean, it's chicken and rice. It's not that deep."

The bell rang. The crowd thinned. As they walked toward homeroom, Jaya pulled out her phone and opened Mira's page.

"Tell me I'm imagining this," she said.

Mira watched the two videos back to back—hers first, then his. Same steps. Same sequence. Even the title was similar. Her words were quieter, the camera wobbly. His was all precision and confidence.

"Maybe it's just… coincidence," she said, though she didn't quite believe it.

"He follows you," Jaya pointed out. "He liked your banana bread clip last month. He definitely saw this."

Mira didn't respond. Her heart felt oddly heavy for something so small. It wasn't that she wanted five thousand likes. She wasn't planning on building a channel. But watching her quiet, useful thing turned into someone else's highlight reel felt like someone had taken a conversation meant for her kitchen and put it on a billboard with their face on it.

"You should call him out," Jaya said. "Or at least comment something."

"And say what? 'You cooked food that I also cooked'?"

"Say, 'Nice recreation, inspired by the original.'"

Mira shook her head. "I don't want to start anything. It's just a recipe."

Jaya scowled. "It's not *just* a recipe. It's your way of caring for people. That should count for something."

They reached the classroom door. Mira adjusted her glasses, trying to swallow the knot in her throat.

"Maybe it does," she said. "Just not in the way the internet counts."

Throughout the day, Levi's video followed her like an echo. It popped up on other people's screens during study hall. The girl sitting two rows over in math showed it to their teacher, who nodded appreciatively and said, "Looks good," without knowing she was praising someone else's copy.

By lunch, a few kids were calling him "Chef" like it was a new nickname. He took the teasing with a grin, half-protesting, half-accepting the title.

Mira picked at her sandwich, appetite dulled.

"You know what's wild?" Jaya said, scrolling. "Half of these comments are about his editing, not the food. Look. 'The transitions ate.' 'You should teach a class on lighting.' 'The camera work is insane.'"

Mira leaned over. It was true. People commented on how clean his kitchen looked, how crisp the sound was when the chicken hit the pan, how nice his countertop marble was. No one mentioned the actual flavor.

She thought about her own comments—two from people who knew her, who might someday ask for a bowl when they were sick or tired. No one had shared her video. No one had called her a chef. But if Ms. Dollard knocked on her door tomorrow and asked for help making soup, Mira would show up. Maybe that was the difference.

"You ever feel like this place is allergic to quiet?" Mira asked.

"School or the internet?" Jaya said.

"Both."

"All the time."

They sat in comfortable silence for a moment. The cafeteria roared around them, kids filming, laughing, yelling across tables.

"Hey," Jaya said suddenly. "Look at this."

She'd switched apps without really thinking about it, her thumb moving on muscle memory more than intent. A thread surfaced in her explore feed—disconnected posts stitched together by irritation rather than agreement. People complained about paid reviews, exaggerated routines, creators recommending things they clearly didn't use. Some posts came with screenshots, others with sarcasm, still others with sprawling comment sections full of people arguing past one another.

One post read, I miss when people just shared things because they liked them.

Another snapped back, That time never existed. You just didn't know how the sausage was made.

Someone else added, Everything feels fake now, followed immediately by a reply insisting, Nothing's changed—people just want to feel smarter than the algorithm.

The comments didn't line up. They contradicted each other, overlapped, doubled back. No consensus formed—just noise.

Jaya leaned over Mira's shoulder, squinting at the screen. "Wow. Everybody's mad but nobody agrees on what they're mad about."

Mira scrolled slowly. She didn't feel vindicated or validated by what she saw. If anything, the chaos made her feel smaller, like she'd wandered into an argument already halfway over and missed the beginning. Everyone seemed to be shouting about truth while using filters, sarcasm, and half-context to make their point.

"It's like the internet doesn't know what it wants to be," Jaya said. "Helpful? Entertaining? Honest? Famous?"

Mira paused on a comment buried three layers down. No emojis. No flair.

I don't need someone influencing me. I need someone showing me how something actually works.

She didn't like it because it felt prophetic or bold. She liked it because it sounded tired. Practical. Like someone who'd stopped expecting the internet to fix anything and just wanted it to be useful.

"That one," Mira said, tilting the screen slightly so Jaya could see. "That makes sense."

Jaya read it and nodded. "Yeah. That feels... normal."

Mira locked her phone and set it face-down on the table. Whatever people decided to call real out there—online, in comment sections, in trending audio—it didn't line up with what she felt standing at the stove last night, chopping vegetables in a quiet kitchen while her cat watched like a veteran supervisor.

She wasn't trying to be part of a movement. She didn't feel like she belonged to a side. All she knew was that what she made had a purpose, even if it only reached two people and a cat.

"That internet stuff will change again next week," Jaya said, stuffing her phone into her pocket. "It always does."

Mira nodded. She believed that part.

What didn't change—what hadn't changed since she was little—was the way her chest settled when something was done right, even if no one noticed. The way usefulness felt steadier than praise. The way quiet effort didn't ask to be named.

That wasn't a trend.
It was just how she knew how to live.

That evening, after homework and a quick check on the garden, Mira sat at the small desk in her room, phone in hand. Levi's video had crossed fifty thousand views. Hers had stalled at maybe twenty.

Auntie Dee had commented again: **next time I'm over, we're making this together. I'll bring the rolls.**

Ms. Dollard had added a small follow-up: **I made a version with what I had in my pantry. Turned out pretty good. Thank you, dear.**

Someone with a username she didn't recognize—just a string of numbers—had liked the video without commenting. That was fine. Not everything needed words.

She clicked over to Levi's page for one more look. The top comment now read: **I swear you're the only one I trust on here, everything you make looks legit.**

Mira locked her phone.

Professor Butterbean hopped up onto the desk, nearly knocking a stack of library books to the floor. He settled himself partly on her notebook, partly on her forearm, effectively trapping her.

"You think I should be mad?" she asked him.

He blinked slowly.

"Because I'm… not, exactly. Just tired."

He responded by headbutting her wrist until she scratched his cheek.

She pulled her arm free, opened her journal, and wrote one simple line near the bottom of the page:

Being first is not the same as being true.

She sat with the words for a moment.

Out in the world, numbers kept climbing on a video that wasn't really his idea. Trends would keep trending. People would keep copying. Algorithms would keep mistaking loud for important.

In her notebook, the sentence just sat there, quiet and solid.

It didn't feel like much.

But it felt real.

CHAPTER FOUR

The Elephant Drawer

Not everything that endures asks to be noticed.

Mira had always known which drawer it was.

Even before she could reach the top of the dresser without standing on the bed, she knew exactly where her mother kept it—second from the bottom, right side, the one that stuck just a little when you pulled it open too fast. For years, Delilah had kept it out of reach, not because it was secret or forbidden, but because Mira was gentle to a fault and the things inside were not all durable.

By fourteen, Mira was beyond tall enough to open it herself.

She did so now, standing in her room with the door half-closed, the late-afternoon sun sliding through the blinds in thin, golden bands that fell across the carpet and the edge of her desk. Professor Butterbean lounged on the windowsill, one paw hanging lazily over the side, eyes half-lidded as if the world outside were more suggestion than requirement.

The drawer opened with a soft resistance.

Inside was a small, careful chaos.

It wasn't filled to the brim, nor arranged with any obvious order. Things lay side by side because they belonged together, not because they matched. A wooden elephant sat near the front—dark and polished, its trunk curved upward, one ear chipped from the time Mira dropped it while dusting. Near it were two smooth stones, one gray and one pink, wrapped together in a strip of faded ribbon. Beneath them rested a folded piece of paper, creased so many times it no longer held shape without effort.

Mira lifted the paper first. She unfolded it slowly, already knowing what it said.

Thank you for sitting with him. He doesn't talk anymore, but he was calmer today.

It was written in shaky handwriting, signed only with an initial. Mira had found the note slipped into her backpack after volunteering at the assisted living center with her mother three summers ago. She hadn't told anyone about it—hadn't known why it felt important, only that it did. So she kept it.

She folded it again and placed it back where it belonged.

The elephant figurines came next. There were six in total, each different. The wooden one had been a gift from Delilah after Mira read an entire library book about African wildlife in third grade. The glass one—a translucent blue with bubbles frozen inside—had been found at a thrift store during one of their Saturday wanderings, when Delilah was tired but trying anyway.

"That one looks like you," her mother had said, holding it up to the light. "Solid, but letting the sun through."

Mira hadn't known how to respond to that, so she'd just nodded.

Another elephant was ceramic, painted in faded white with tiny cracks along its back. Mira had fixed those with glue herself, the seam still visible if you knew where to look. Two more were rubbery and clearly meant as toys, their edges worn smooth by hands that had pressed them during nervous moments.

The smallest one—a bronze charm no bigger than her thumbnail—rested in the corner of the drawer, separated slightly from the others. It had been sewn once into the lining of a jacket no longer in her closet.

Mira touched it gently.

It was a strange thing, this quiet attraction she'd always felt toward elephants. Not because they were cute—she knew better than that. Elephants were massive, slow-moving, capable of great force. They mourned their dead. They remembered wrongs and kindnesses with equal clarity. They were social creatures who somehow still carried solitude with dignity.

They felt… honest.

Mira had read once that elephants could recognize themselves in mirrors. That fact had stayed with her longer than most.

She leaned back against her bed, drawer still open, and let her thoughts drift the way they rarely did during the noise of a school day. This was her quiet time. Not naps—she never napped—but this small pocket of stillness where the world stopped demanding explanations.

Her phone lay face-up on the desk, screen lighting briefly with a new notification before dimming again. She didn't look.

Down the street, she heard laughter. Someone shouting. A car door slamming.

"Loud borders," Alina had said earlier in the week. Mira smiled faintly at the memory. She wondered if Alina had a drawer too. Or if her important things lived elsewhere—stitched into backpacks or pressed between notebook pages.

Mira closed the elephant drawer softly and slid it back in.

She'd barely turned around when her phone buzzed again, more insistently this time.

Trending: ChefLevi

She frowned and picked it up against her better judgment.

Levi's video had doubled again. New comments filled the screen faster than she could read them. Someone had stitched it. Someone else had duetted, mimicking his movements exactly, replacing the cooking with exaggerated gestures and jokes.

A parody of a copy of an imitation.

Mira blinked and locked the phone without commenting.

She didn't feel angry—at least, not in the way people expected anger to feel. There was no heat, no urge to respond. Instead, she felt something quieter and more persistent, like a low pressure behind her sternum.

Useful things didn't have to shout.

She pushed the chair at her desk back and opened her homework planner, flipping to tomorrow's assignments. Algebra worksheet. Reading chapter twelve. Volunteer schedule confirmation for Saturday.

She paused at the last one.

Downstairs, Delilah was on the phone talking in that calm, practiced voice she used for scheduling and reassurance. Mira could hear her mother's steps moving from kitchen to hallway, the muffled sound of drawers opening and closing.

"Saturday's fine," Delilah said. "We can bring muffins again."

Mira closed the planner.

"Mom?" she called.

"Yes, baby?"

"I can bake instead of muffins. The banana bread recipe. I can double it."

There was a pause, then the sound of relief curling through her mother's voice. "That would be wonderful. Thank you."

Mira smiled to herself.

She moved downstairs, pulling ingredients from the pantry without turning lights on. The kitchen was warm now, the sun angling through the window above the sink. Professor Butterbean followed her automatically, hopping onto the chair near the counter, tail swaying like a metronome.

Before touching anything else, Mira went to the sink and washed her hands. Not rushed, not fussy—just the way she always did it. Warm water first, then soap, scrubbing palms, backs of hands, fingertips. She rinsed, dried them on the clean towel hanging from the oven handle, then paused for half a second, breathing in the quiet. Ready.

She cracked eggs. Mashed bananas. Measured flour by feel as much as by cup.

She didn't film this time.

Sometimes cooking was meant to be shared. Sometimes it was meant to be given. And sometimes, Mira thought, it was simply meant to be done.

As the bread baked, filling the house with sweetness, Mira wiped the counter clean and took the finished loaf upstairs once it cooled enough to handle. She set it beside the elephant drawer, the smell of it mingling faintly with old wood and paper.

When she opened the drawer again, she added something new.

A small sticky note, torn from her planner, written carefully:

Baked. Didn't post. Still mattered.

She folded it once and placed it beside the wooden elephant.

The drawer closed.

On Saturday morning, the assisted living center was quieter than the school hallways but louder than Mira's house. Televisions murmured from open doorways. A radio played something old and soft near the nurses' station. Laughter surfaced now and then, brief and unguarded, before settling back into the general hum. Utensils clinked against plates. Someone coughed. Someone sang to themselves under their breath.

Delilah had been volunteering here for as long as Mira could remember—long enough that the receptionist greeted her by first name, long enough that some of the residents expected her on Saturdays the way they once expected church on Sundays. It wasn't something she talked about much. It was just something she did.

At first, when Mira was younger, she had assumed this was simply what families did: you helped where you could, especially where people were lonely. Only later did she realize that not everyone thought that way. Some people considered volunteering a phase, or a line for college applications, or a favor done once a year when guilt surfaced at convenient times.

For Delilah, it was steadier than that.

Before Mira existed, before the house on Birchwood Lane, before the hospital job and the careful routines, Delilah had been younger and softer in ways that weren't visible anymore. She had believed very hard in people, even when they hadn't earned it. Especially when they hadn't earned it. She had mistaken intensity for passion, control for certainty, charm for goodness.

Mira hadn't learned the details all at once. They came in fragments over the years—things Delilah let surface only when Mira was old enough to hold them without dropping.

Her father had not always been cruel. That was the part Delilah struggled most to explain. In the beginning, he had been magnetic. Certain. Fully present, as long as things went his way. He spoke in absolutes, right and wrong, loyalty and betrayal, love and punishment. There were no soft edges to him, no gray places. Everything was cleanly divided, as if the world itself ran on rules only he could see.

Mira's birth changed something. Delilah never knew precisely what. Perhaps the pressure cracked something that was already brittle. Perhaps jealousy crept in where devotion once lived. Or perhaps whatever he had been hiding—anger, addiction, illness—could no longer stay buried once responsibility arrived.

The first incident Delilah ever spoke of was the easiest to tell.

She had burned dinner. Nothing dramatic. Just distracted, too tired, too new at motherhood to notice the smell in time. He'd slammed the plate into the sink so hard it chipped, then accused her of disrespect. Of ingratitude. Of trying to embarrass him.

Mira had been asleep in the next room.

The second was quieter but worse.

She'd questioned where he'd been. Just a question. He'd leaned in close enough that she could smell something sharp and unfamiliar on his breath, and told her—calmly—that asking questions was how women destroyed their families. His hand had wrapped around her wrist, fingers tight enough to bruise but careful not to leave marks where anyone might see.

The third was the one Delilah never described in detail. Only that Mira had been in her arms when he shouted. Only that his voice had filled the room like weather, unpredictable and threatening. Only that something in Delilah had finally gone still.

That stillness frightened her more than the yelling ever had.

She never found proof of what she suspected. No bottles hidden, no bags, nothing obvious. But the shifts were too sharp, too complete. One moment loving, the next cruel. Devotion turning absolute and then flipping into contempt. She wondered if it was addiction. She wondered if it was illness. She wondered if it was simply the kind of person he'd always been, finally unmasked.

She stopped wondering when Mira was nine months old.

By then, she had learned his routines. The nights he disappeared. The hours he was least likely to notice details. She packed a bag slowly, over time, hiding essentials beneath folded clothes. Money tucked into books. Diapers stacked behind towels.

She waited.

One night, when he left the apartment the same way he always did, Delilah took Mira, locked the door behind her, and never came back.

They stayed with a church friend at first. Then a cousin. Then another friend whose name Mira never remembered. Delilah worked whatever hours she could, took night shifts, learned how to live with less before less ever demanded it. She learned how to listen for warning signs instead of ignoring them. She learned that love without gentleness was not love at all.

Faith entered her life again not as performance or certainty, but as shelter. Quiet prayers whispered over a sleeping baby. Scriptures read more as reminders than rules. A God large enough to hold unanswered questions and still offer safety.

A year later, Delilah received a call.

Mira's father had been killed in an accident.

That was all anyone could tell her. That he was gone. That it was sudden. That there were no details anyone seemed willing—or able—to confirm. She asked questions and received the same non-answers until she stopped asking.

She knew he was truly dead. The paperwork confirmed that. The silence afterward made it clear.

What she never had was a full story. What happened. Why. Whether substances were involved. Whether he'd been alone. Whether, in the end, he'd found peace or simply stopped running.

Delilah grieved him in pieces. Not for who he was, but for who he never became. Not for the life she lost, but for the danger she escaped.

Volunteering followed not long after.

At first, it wasn't intentional. She had accompanied a friend once, then filled in another time when someone couldn't make it. She noticed how safe these hallways felt. How predictably kind the work was. How no one raised their voice. How listening mattered more than speaking.

Giving back became a way of reminding herself—and eventually Mira—that suffering did not get the final word. That people could be vulnerable without being dangerous. That care could be simple and steady without strings.

Mira had grown up in those spaces. Passing out baked goods. Sitting quietly beside people who didn't want conversation but didn't want to be alone. Learning, without being told, that attention could be an act of love.

Delilah was generous by nature, but Mira carried that softness further. Where Delilah had learned discernment through pain, Mira seemed to begin there naturally. She gave freely, but carefully. Helped instinctively, but without needing credit. She absorbed the world deeply, then responded to it with gentleness instead of reaction.

Delilah saw it and worried sometimes. But she also trusted it.

Now, at fourteen, Mira walked these halls with a steadiness that belied her age.

Mira navigated the hallway slowly, balancing a box of banana bread slices with practiced care.

“Miss Mira!” Mrs. Howell called from her room, waving a hand thin as paper. “Is that yours?”

“Yes, ma’am,” Mira said. “I tried not to overdo the sugar.”

Mrs. Howell sniffed approvingly. “Good. I like to taste the bread, not the regret.”

Mira laughed and stepped inside, setting the box down on the small table near the window. Another resident watched quietly from a chair, hands folded, eyes unreadable.

“When did you get so tall?” Mrs. Howell asked.

“Slowly,” Mira said.

“Well, you did it politely,” Mrs. Howell declared. “That counts.”

As Mira sliced and served, she listened more than she spoke. Stories drifted through the room—small recollections, half-finished thoughts, fragments of memory that sometimes tangled and sometimes settled. Mira nodded and asked questions when they felt welcome.

She noticed things. Who needed more time to chew. Who avoided eye contact. Who smiled only when spoken to directly.

No one filmed.

The moment felt full anyway.

Later, as she walked back toward the exit, Mira passed the bulletin board near the reception desk. Flyers overlapped in layers: bingo night, exercise class, visiting hours.

One hand-written note caught her eye.

Thank you to the volunteers who see us.

No names were listed.

Mira tightened her grip on the empty box.

At home that evening, she sat in her room again, legs folded beneath her, phone on the bed beside her. Jaya had sent her six messages—memes, screenshots, angry commentary about Levi's latest brand deal inquiry.

Mira read them without replying.

She opened her journal instead.

Sometimes she wrote full pages. Sometimes single sentences. Tonight, she drew a small elephant in the margin, trunk raised, feet planted firmly.

Underneath, she wrote:

Not everything that moves fast moves forward.

She didn't know why she wrote it. She only knew it was true.

The phone buzzed again.

This time, the notification wasn't from school or social media.

It was an email.

Subject line: **Community Garden Recognition — Inquiry**

Mira frowned, heartbeat quickening just a little.

She didn't open it yet.

Instead, she slid open the elephant drawer one more time, as if checking to make sure it was still there. The figurines sat patiently, unchanged.

She closed the drawer.

CHAPTER FIVE

A Bouquet for Ms. Dollard

Some lives measure their worth by what they keep. Others by what they give away.

Mira waited until the bread had cooled completely before wrapping it.

She cut the loaf carefully, each slice even, not because anyone would count them but because it felt right that way. The crust yielded with a quiet crackle beneath the knife, still warm enough at the center to release steam. She arranged the slices in the small white box Delilah saved specifically for baking—clean, sturdy, reused just often enough to feel familiar.

The tulips came next.

They were not all fully open yet. Two were still tight at the edges, color pressed inward like a held breath. Mira preferred them that way. Flowers that bloomed too fast never seemed to last as long.

She tied the bundle with twine from the drawer beneath the sink, looping it once, then adjusting so the knot sat a little to the side. Balanced, but not formal.

Professor Butterbean watched the entire process from the counter with grave seriousness.

"These aren't for you," Mira told him gently.

He blinked, unconvinced.

Outside, the air had softened compared to earlier in the week. The sun filtered through thin clouds, the light pale and even, the kind that didn't rush anyone. Mira slipped on her jacket, tucked the box of banana bread under one arm, and picked up the tulips with her free hand.

Ms. Dollard's house sat two doors down, a small blue ranch with white trim that had faded into something closer to ivory over time. The porch rail slanted slightly to the left, as if settling into a preferred posture after years of standing straight. Wind chimes hung near the door, glass and metal pieces clinking softly whenever a breeze passed through.

Mira knocked once, then stepped back the way Delilah had taught her—far enough to be polite, close enough not to feel absent.

It took a moment.

She heard footsteps before the door opened, slow but deliberate.

"Well, look at you," Ms. Dollard said, smiling wide. "If you aren't the best surprise I've had all week."

Her voice carried a rasp Mira recognized, the kind that came with years of careful use rather than damage. Ms. Dollard stood just taller than Mira's shoulder, wrapped in a soft cardigan that had been washed so often it had lost all stiffness. Her hair—once dark, Mira had been told—was now a silver that caught the light like thread.

"For me?" Ms. Dollard asked, eyeing the tulips.

"Yes, ma'am," Mira said. "And bread. Banana."

Ms. Dollard stepped aside immediately. "You've come to the right house, then."

The living room smelled faintly of tea and old paper, a warm, settled smell. Books lined the shelves—hardbacks mostly, their spines creased but intact. Framed photographs covered the mantel: two children at various ages, stiff-haired school portraits that progressed into wedding photos, and finally a set of holiday pictures taken in the same spot year after year.

Mira set the bread on the small table near the couch while Ms. Dollard took the tulips to the kitchen and found a vase already waiting on the counter.

"You timed these beautifully," she said, trimming the stems with careful precision. "I always say flowers should look like they're still deciding whether to show off."

Mira smiled. "That's how they were when I cut them."

"Smart flowers," Ms. Dollard said. "They'll do just fine here."

They settled at the kitchen table with tea and bread. Ms. Dollard insisted on plates, warming the slices slightly in the toaster oven "so they'd remember what they're meant to be." Mira watched the older woman move around the kitchen with ease, every motion economical but unhurried.

"You know," Ms. Dollard said, slicing the bread, "your mother could've been anything."

Mira tilted her head. "She is."

Ms. Dollard chuckled. "True. But I meant… the way she listens. That's rare."

Mira nodded. "She learned it."

They ate in comfortable silence for a few moments, punctuated only by the clink of forks and the hum of the kettle cooling.

It wasn't an awkward silence. With some people, quiet felt like something you had to hurry up and fill, tossing in words the way people tossed ice cubes into lukewarm drinks. With Ms. Dollard, silence felt like another form of conversation. Like sitting on a porch watching the sky change colors together and agreeing, without saying anything, that the moment was enough.

Mira's gaze drifted around the living room, the way it always did when she was here. Nothing in Ms. Dollard's house was new, but everything was cared for. The sofa cushions were a little flattened, but the fabric was clean and smelled faintly of lavender. The end tables didn't match, yet both held coasters and neatly stacked books. Her TV was small by everyone else's standards, but the screen was dust-free and the remote was always in the same spot, lined up with almost military precision.

There were pictures on the walls, but not too many. A framed black-and-white wedding photo. Two small school pictures of children who must have been her son and daughter, gap-toothed and smiling in outfits that screamed late '80s. Later, the same two as teens, a little awkward, a little unsure of themselves. In all of them, Ms. Dollard stood or sat slightly to the side, a steady hand on a shoulder, eyes bright, never trying to stand in front.

Mira remembered the first time she'd stepped into this house. She'd been four, so small her backpack looked like it might tip her over. They had just moved into the rental on the corner—"finally ours," Delilah had said, even though it belonged to a landlord and the paint peeled a little near the back door. After three years of sleeping in borrowed rooms, temporary apartments, and once, for two months, on a friend's couch with a curtain hung for privacy, the house on Birchwood Lane had felt like a miracle even before Mira's garden existed.

That first week, everything had been boxes and confusion. The kitchen cabinets were only half-unpacked. The oven smelled strange the first time they turned it on. Mira remembered sitting in the middle of the living room floor, hugging her stuffed elephant, while her mother tried to fix a wobbly leg on the coffee table with a butter knife and a roll of tape.

There had been a knock on the door. Delilah froze for a fraction of a second—a reflex left over from the years when knocks meant landlords with questions or police with bad news. Then she pasted on a polite smile and opened it.

"Hello?" she'd said cautiously.

On the stoop stood a woman in a denim shirt and soft gray pants, holding a square glass dish covered in foil. Her hair, already mostly white, was pulled back in a clip, and she wore small gold hoop earrings that caught the light when she nodded.

"Afternoon," the woman had said. "I'm your neighbor from next door. Name's Dollard. I figured if someone just moved in, they probably don't feel like cooking tonight. This is nothing fancy, just baked ziti and a salad, but it's dinner."

Delilah's face had done something complicated then—relief and surprise and a reluctance to accept kindness all at once. Mira remembered watching from the floor as her mother stepped back, invited her in, and repeated "thank you" at least three times in a row.

It was later that week, when Delilah's sitter for an overtime shift fell through, that Ms. Dollard became more than "the lady next door." Mira could still picture it: her mother kneeling in front of her, hands on her small shoulders.

"I have to go in tonight," Delilah had said, voice strained. "Ms. Janice can't watch you. But Ms. Dollard offered, remember? The one who brought the baked ziti? You liked her."

"She had cookies," four-year-old Mira had pointed out solemnly.

"She did have cookies," Delilah agreed, a little smile breaking through. "I wouldn't leave you with anyone I didn't trust, okay?"

Trust was a fragile thing for Delilah back then. But she took a breath, walked next door with Mira's small overnight bag, and knocked again. Ms. Dollard opened the door like she'd been expecting them all her life.

"You go on and work," she'd told Delilah. "She and I are going to read every book I own and maybe eat too many crackers."

It had taken Delilah a full thirty seconds to let go of Mira's hand. But when she did, she looked around Ms. Dollard's living room and saw what Mira would later learn to recognize: low chaos, soft order, a gentleness that came from knowing what truly mattered. The house wasn't filled with expensive things, yet every object had a place. No piles of unopened boxes, no mystery projects half-finished and abandoned in corners. Just a clean floor, a lamp that worked, a blanket folded neatly over the back of the chair where someone might sit to rest.

That night became one of many. Whenever Delilah picked up an extra shift or needed to run an errand without dragging a sleepy child along, she'd knock on Ms. Dollard's door. Sometimes she slipped a twenty-dollar bill into her hand; sometimes she just brought banana bread or a casserole. Ms. Dollard always waved it off at first, then accepted with a kind of practical gratitude.

"She made it easy to breathe in this new place," Delilah had told Mira once. "Like someone had already decided before we got here that this street was allowed to be safe."

Mira thought about that now as she looked around the familiar room. The same lamp that had lit her evening storytimes when she was small still stood beside the armchair. The blanket was a different one—thicker, more worn—but folded just as carefully. The table where they now ate had once been the site of puzzle Lenathons on rainy days. When she was six, Ms. Dollard had taught her how to find the edge pieces first. "Build the frame," she'd said. "Then the middle feels less impossible."

Maybe that was what Ms. Dollard's whole life looked like: edges defined, center filled in slowly, with patience.

Back at the table, Mira watched the older woman slice another piece of banana bread. Her movements were unhurried, but not weak. Every gesture seemed deliberate. Present.

"You know your mama came over that first week y'all moved in and tried to pay me like I was a professional service?" Ms. Dollard said, as if reading her thoughts. "I told her, 'Delilah, I am not a daycare. I'm a neighbor. Let me be that.'"

"I'm glad you did," Mira said. "I don't remember everything from back then, but I remember being here. It felt… quiet. In a good way."

"Well, that's on purpose." Ms. Dollard glanced around her own home with a small, satisfied smile. "I decided a long time ago that I wanted a life where I could hear myself think. No chaos if I can help it. Just enough stuff to be comfortable. Not so much that I can't see what I already have."

"That sounds like my mom," Mira said softly.

"Your mother had to learn it the hard way." Ms. Dollard's voice gentled. "She didn't tell me all the details at first. Just enough so I knew she'd been through something no one deserved. That man of hers… he didn't know what he had."

Mira swallowed. She knew pieces of the story now—how her father's temper had curdled into something darker after she was born, how he'd broken a plate against the wall when Delilah asked about a paycheck that never showed up, how he'd once put his fist through the bedroom door because the baby wouldn't stop crying. How her mother had quietly packed a bag one night after he stormed out, gathered nine-month-old Mira into her arms, and walked away with nothing but a car full of borrowed courage.

"A man who can't tell the difference between power and cruelty is a man on borrowed time," Ms. Dollard said. "Your mama understood that sooner than most. That's why I admire her. She didn't just leave. She rebuilt. And she didn't let bitterness turn her mean. That's rarer than you think."

Mira drew patterns in a crumb on her plate with the tip of her finger. "She doesn't talk about him much."

"She doesn't owe anyone those details," Ms. Dollard said firmly. "What matters is what she chose after. That woman gives more than she keeps, but she's smarter about who she gives it to now." Her gaze softened. "You, for example. She pours into you on purpose. That's one of the reasons I said yes when she asked me to help with you. I could see she wasn't just dropping you off to escape you. She was building something."

Mira felt her throat tighten again, but this time it wasn't sadness. It was something like gratitude, mixed with the quiet weight of being that "something."

"She calls you her guardian angel sometimes," Mira admitted.

"I'm no angel," Ms. Dollard scoffed lightly. "Just somebody who's had time to figure out what does and doesn't matter. But I appreciate the sentiment."

Mira looked around the room again, seeing it now with a different layer. The well-kept floors. The tidy table. The mismatched, well-loved dishes. The absence of anything showy or performative. Everything here felt… decided. Like Ms. Dollard had intentionally chosen a small life and filled it with care instead of chasing a big one filled with noise.

No wonder her mother admired her. No wonder Mira did too.

"Did I ever tell you what I used to do?" Ms. Dollard asked suddenly.

"I know you're retired," Mira said. "But that's all."

Ms. Dollard smiled. "Most people stop there."

She folded her napkin once, then again, aligning the edges by feel.

"I was an archivist," she said. "For nearly forty years. Public records mostly. Family histories. Letters, journals, documentation people never think matters until time tries to erase it."

Mira's hand paused mid-bite.

"Archives aren't glamorous," Ms. Dollard continued. "Nobody claps for them. But when someone wants to know where they come from—when a court needs truth, when a family needs proof, when a story risks being lost—it's what we turn to."

"That sounds important," Mira said quietly.

"It was," Ms. Dollard said. "Still is. Though most folks don't realize it until much later."

She sipped her tea. "I spent my career preserving what was real. Not what was most exciting. Not what sounded best. Just what was true."

Mira felt something shift gently into place inside her, like a drawer closing properly.

"My children used to tease me," Ms. Dollard went on. "Said nobody cared about old papers. Said the future was forward-facing."

She smiled, but there was something tired in it. "They live forward-facing lives now. Busy ones. Very important. They come by in December, when the roads are clear and the calendars allow."

"That must be nice," Mira said, choosing her words carefully.

"It is," Ms. Dollard said, surprising her. "Because they know where I am. And when they need something remembered, they still call."

She leaned back slightly. "But I learned a long time ago not to confuse attention with love."

Mira nodded, thinking of noisy hallways and flashing screens.

"I had peace in my work," Ms. Dollard said. "Not fame. Not applause. Peace. I went home at night knowing I had preserved something honest."

She gestured toward the vase of tulips. "This is the same kind of work. Just looks different."

They finished the bread. Ms. Dollard wrapped the remaining slices with care and placed them on the counter.

"You'll take some back," she said, not asking.

"Yes, ma'am."

Ms. Dollard rose slowly and walked to the bookshelf, scanning the rows until she found what she was looking for. She pulled out a slim volume and brought it to the table.

"Here," she said. "I want you to have this."

Mira accepted it carefully. The cover read: *Collected Letters, 1918–1943.*

"These were written by ordinary people," Ms. Dollard said. "None of them knew they'd be remembered. But every one of them mattered."

Mira nodded, throat tight.

As she stood to leave, Ms. Dollard touched her wrist gently. “You don’t rush,” she said. “That’s a gift. Don’t let anyone tell you otherwise.”

“I won’t,” Mira promised.

Outside, the afternoon light had shifted, warmer now, gold brushing the edges of everything.

As Mira walked back toward her house, the phone in her pocket buzzed once. She didn’t check it.

Behind her, Ms. Dollard stood for a moment longer than necessary, watching the tall girl walk away with her careful step, bread box tucked under her arm, tulips replaced by memory.

Not everything valuable announced itself.

Some things simply endured.

PART II

PRESSURE

CHAPTER SIX

The Day It Arrived

Some things fall without warning, but not without reason.

It happened on a Tuesday.

Not the dramatic kind of Tuesday that storms in with headlines or announcements over the intercom. Just an ordinary one—spirit week halfway over, hallway glitter still clinging to the floors, cafeteria serving square pizza that tasted like memory more than food.

That was why it caught everyone off guard.

The email arrived during third period.

Ms. Brantley was mid-sentence, explaining something about independent project deadlines, when a gasp rippled through the room like a dropped glass. Phones appeared under desks. Screens tilted toward neighbors. Someone whispered a name, sharp and disbelieving.

"No way."

"That's fake."

"There's no application out yet."

Ms. Brantley paused. She'd learned to recognize the particular hum of distraction that meant something had spread faster than she could redirect it.

"Okay," she said carefully. "What's going on?"

No one answered her directly, but someone turned their phone face-up on the desk between two chairs. The subject line was visible from halfway across the room.

Congratulations on Your Selection.

The recipient was a junior—not even in Mira's grade. A quiet kid from the other side of the building. Smart, but not loud about it. Known more for keeping to himself than for posting anything memorable online.

The Tether Emerging Creators Scholarship.

Awarded.

Confirmed.

Finalized.

Without an application.

Ms. Brantley took the phone when it reached her desk. She read the email once. Then again. Her mouth tightened—not in suspicion, but in genuine confusion.

“Well,” she said slowly, “that’s… unexpected.”

The bell rang before she could say anything else.

And just like that, the day tipped.

By lunch, the story had splintered into versions.

Some people said the recipient had been scouted early. Others claimed his family had connections. One rumor insisted it was a clerical error that would be corrected by the end of the day. A more hopeful theory floated around social media: maybe the school district was experimenting with a new process—something more… organic.

TikTok exploded.

Reaction videos. Guessing threads. Fake acceptance emails posted for engagement. People dug through the kid’s old posts, trying to reverse-engineer whatever had gotten him chosen.

“See?” someone said, pointing at a blurry video from two years earlier. “He *did* post drawings. That’s gotta be it.”

“No,” another argued. “Look at this one—he volunteered at that renovation thing over the summer.”

"Maybe they're tracking consistency," someone else said. "Like… growth over time."

Mira watched all of this from the edge of the cafeteria table, unbothered by the noise but attentive in her own quiet way. She didn't feel envy. If anything, she felt the mild, persistent itch of curiosity—the same feeling she got when a plant sprouted somewhere she hadn't expected.

Jaya slid into the seat beside her, phone still glowing. "Okay. Thoughts?"

Mira frowned slightly, thinking. "It doesn't feel random."

"That's what I said."

"But it doesn't feel… strategic either," Mira added. "If it were strategy, people would recognize it."

Jaya tilted her head. "So what does it feel like?"

Mira hesitated. She wasn't sure how to describe it.

"Like timing," she said finally. "Like the moment matched the person."

Jaya blinked. "You sound like Ms. Dollard."

Mira smiled faintly and picked at her apple slices.

The rest of the day passed in fragments—teachers distracted, students restless, administrators moving a little too quickly through the halls with folders tucked tightly to their chests. Every screen hummed with speculation.

By the time Mira reached home, the internet had already begun categorizing the scholarship recipient.

Lucky.
Privileged.
Rigged.
Deserving—maybe.

People were very good at assigning cause when confronted with effect.

She set her backpack down by the stairs and kicked off her sneakers, lining them up without thinking. Professor Butterbean appeared immediately, winding around her ankles as if she'd been gone far longer than a school day.

"I know," she murmured, crouching to scratch his chin. "It was loud out there."

The house was quiet in the way that belonged to weekday afternoons—sunlight slouched across the kitchen floor, the hum of the refrigerator a steady presence. Delilah wouldn't be home for another hour at least.

Mira washed her hands at the sink, letting the water run a few seconds longer than necessary. The routine grounded her, steadied the leftover noise from the day. When she finished, she dried them carefully and leaned against the counter.

Only then did she check her phone again.

The unread email from last Thursday night waited where she'd left it.

Subject: Community Garden Recognition — Inquiry

Her chest tightened—not with excitement, exactly. More like… attentive alertness. The same feeling she got when a plant behaved differently than expected. Not wrong. Just notable.

She hadn't opened it over the weekend. She tried to keep not urgent matters like random emails to a minimum on the weekends. Then, after the Sunday hang-out, Ms. Dollard's words had still been sitting heavy in her chest. The bread. The drawer. The day had felt full in a way she didn't want to rush.

Now, standing alone in the kitchen, it felt like the right moment.

Mira didn't open it immediately.

Instead, she walked upstairs and pulled open the elephant drawer one more time—not out of superstition, but reassurance. The figurines sat exactly as they always had. Steady. Unconcerned. Silent witnesses to nothing and everything.

She closed the drawer.

Then she returned downstairs, sat at the table, and opened the email.

The message was formal, almost old-fashioned in tone.

It referenced the neighborhood garden project. Mentioned "consistent stewardship." Used phrases like *long-term care* and *community impact* without once referencing grades, followers, or visibility.

They wanted to talk.

Not congratulate her.
Not announce anything.
Just… ask questions.

Mira read it twice. Then a third time.

There was no request for a portfolio. No link to submit videos. No prompt to document her work. Just an invitation to respond if she was willing to share more about her role in maintaining the garden and her interest in community-based projects.

She stared at the screen until the words softened around the edges.

It wasn't an opportunity yet.
It wasn't a rejection.
It wasn't even a reward.

It was recognition.

That unsettled her more than she expected.

Recognition carried weight. Expectations. Direction.

The scholarship story from earlier that day floated back into her mind, uninvited.

Someone else's name. Someone else's inbox lighting up without warning.

She didn't feel jealous of that student. She felt… aligned and misaligned at the same time. Like two clocks ticking on the same wall, both correct, but marking different kinds of time.

Mira set her phone face-down on the table.

She didn't reply yet.

The community garden wasn't something Mira talked about much.

Not because it was secret, but because it had never felt like a talking thing. It was just… there. Like gravity. Like breathing.

She'd found it five years ago, when she was nine.

That was the summer Delilah finally signed a lease-to-own with her name on it — their first true house after years of borrowed rooms, short stays, and waiting lists. The garden sat three blocks away, tucked between an auto repair shop and an old community center whose paint peeled in patient strips. At first glance, it looked abandoned: rotting wooden beds, a chain-link gate tied shut with wire, weeds tall enough to hide a child.

Mira remembered standing at the fence that day, fingers wrapped around the metal, squinting through heat shimmer and overgrowth.

"It's dead," Delilah had said gently, already pulling her along toward home.

But Mira had shaken her head. "No," she'd said. "It's just quiet."

Quiet, it turned out, was correct.

The garden had been started years earlier by a church group that lost members, funding, momentum — the way good things sometimes do when no one is there to tend them consistently. The soil was still rich underneath the neglect. Mira felt it the first day she climbed through the crooked gate with gloves three sizes too big and began pulling weeds with stubborn focus.

Delilah hadn't stopped her. She brought water. Then tools. Then compost someone from the volunteer center donated once they realized someone was actually caring for the space again.

By the end of that first summer, two beds were cleared.

Only two.

Mira hadn't tried to revive everything. She never did things that way. She focused on what she could manage, gave it attention, and let the results decide the next step.

That became her pattern.

Over five seasons, the garden grew — not explosively, but faithfully.

Spring crops first: collard greens, kale, spinach, lettuce, radishes. Tomatoes trained carefully onto salvaged cages once the frost passed. Peppers in neat rows — bell, banana, jalapeño. Zucchini that always seemed to overproduce no matter how carefully she planned. Okra that reached skyward by July like it had somewhere important to be.

Fruit bushes followed. Blueberries that took patience and pruning. Strawberries that spread enthusiastically once established. A single dwarf peach tree donated by a retired groundskeeper who said, "You take care of things like they matter."

She did.

Mira learned what thrived in North Carolina heat and what needed shade. She learned rotation without thinking of it as strategy. She learned that plants responded to consistency more than creativity.

By her third successful season, there was more food than she knew what to do with.

So she started giving it away.

First to Ms. Dollard, who lived close enough to walk to the garden with a sturdy cane and a knowing smile. Then to the volunteer center, which quietly welcomed produce without asking for explanation. Later, to the less fortunate kids at school whose backpacks sometimes felt heavier than their lunches.

By the fourth season, Mira was the unofficial manager — not by title, but by gravity. A few neighbors helped when they could. One fixed the broken shed door one afternoon without being asked. Mrs. Hanley down the street watered on days Mira stayed late at school. Someone donated mulch. Someone else left seed packets on the gate.

No announcements were made.
No social media posts.
No signs claiming ownership.

And the harvest kept coming.

Some weeks, there was so much zucchini and tomato that Delilah joked they'd need a second refrigerator. On those weekends, Mira set up a small folding table at the farmers market with a handwritten sign listing prices lower than anyone else's.

She never tried to sell out.

She always did.

People remarked on it every time.

"How do you get so much?"
"What fertilizer is this?"
"Are you sure you planted enough?"

Mira never had a satisfying answer.

She planted seeds.
She tended.
She watered.

She noticed problems early instead of dramatically.
She let things grow.

That was it.

And now, someone had noticed in return.

She looked back at the email.

Recognition.

The word sat strangely in her chest — heavier than praise, lighter than obligation. It wasn't applause. It was acknowledgment.

Mira leaned back in her chair, staring at the ceiling as Professor Butterbean leapt onto the table and curled beside her arm.

She thought of the scholarship kid.
The panic online.
The sudden rush to copy visible goodness.

The garden had never needed an audience. It never asked Mira to explain herself. It just responded.

Her phone buzzed faintly with another round of notifications she ignored.

Instead, she opened her email again and reread the message slowly.

This time, she understood why it unsettled her.

Because it confirmed something she'd always suspected but never named.

What you tended over time mattered more than what you showed all at once.

And that truth was beginning to surface.

That evening, Delilah listened as Mira recounted the day while chopping vegetables for dinner.

"The scholarship one?" Delilah asked. "I heard whispers at work. People love a mystery."

"It unsettled everyone," Mira said. "They're trying to figure out what he did *right*."

Delilah nodded, thoughtful. "People always assume success is earned the loudest."

Mira hesitated, then mentioned the email.

Delilah paused mid-chop. "What kind of inquiry?"

"About the community garden. They said 'recognition.' But it doesn't feel… official."

Delilah wiped her hands on a towel and leaned against the counter. She didn't smile. She didn't celebrate. She didn't caution either.

"That sounds like someone noticing without trying to impress you," she said. "Those are usually the conversations that matter."

"So I should answer?" Mira asked.

Delilah tilted her head. "Do you want to talk about the garden?"

"Yes."

"Then answer."

That was all.

The next day at school, the scholarship chaos hadn't died down. If anything, it had grown teeth.

People filmed reaction videos dissecting the recipient's past. Old posts resurfaced, reframed as proof of destiny or manipulation, depending on the narrator. More than a few students began posting "throwback" clips, reframing half-finished projects as lifelong passions.

Mira noticed the shift.

It wasn't malicious—not yet. More frantic than cruel. Like people who sensed a rule had changed and were scrambling to locate the new one.

In the hallway, she nearly ran into him—a boy she knew but didn't know well.

There was one person Mira never saw at the community garden, yet she always felt his presence in the work he left behind. Eli Jameson—quiet, understated, careful not to take up space he didn't believe belonged to him—had become the garden's invisible backbone long before anyone acknowledged it.

Most people at school knew Eli because of the forearm crutches he used, or because he'd spent the better part of elementary school recovering from a long string of leg surgeries. People noticed the hardware before they noticed the person. But the garden told a different story about him. A true one.

He never crossed paths with Mira there, almost on purpose. If she arrived early, she'd find evidence he had already come and gone: a newly tightened hinge on the gate, the hose bib repaired after weeks of leaking, the compost-bin latch fixed without being asked. Once, she'd discovered an entire row of tomato stakes replaced with ones that didn't wobble in the wind.

He always left the tools wiped clean. Returned exactly where they belonged. Not a single note. Not a claim. Not a hint that he wanted recognition.

Mira didn't comment on it. She simply worked around the improvements, quietly grateful. She understood that some people gave because it was who they were, not because anyone might be watching.

In truth, Eli seemed carved from the same material she lived by—steady effort, no spotlight, no audience required. There was something deeply grounding about knowing someone else cared enough about the garden to keep it whole, even if they never spoke about it.

Some kids made noise to prove they existed. Eli built proof into the soil and left before the sun was fully up.

And Mira noticed. Even if he never knew she did.

They'd worked together once on a science project, and he'd impressed her with how quietly thorough he was.

"Sorry," she said automatically.

"No worries," he replied, smiling. "It's loud lately."

"It is," she agreed.

He adjusted his grip on the crutches. "People are… pivoting."

That made her laugh. "That's one word for it."

"I stopped posting," Eli added, almost casually. "It felt too noisy."

"You build models," Mira said. "The mechanical ones."

He blinked, surprised. "You noticed?"

"I notice," she said simply.

He smiled wider at that, something easing behind his eyes. "Good. Because I kind of like keeping them off-camera."

They parted without ceremony.

Mira carried that interaction with her longer than most.

That night, she sat at her desk and opened the garden email again.

She didn't overthink her response.

She wrote honestly. About dirt under her nails. About learning patience the long way. About Ms. Dollard and the difference it made to be fed without being recorded. About tending soil without expecting applause.

She didn't frame it as achievement.
She framed it as care.

When she finished, she reread it once. Then she sent it.

No flourish. No emojis.

Just truth.

By Friday, the district still hadn't clarified the scholarship process. No corrections were issued. No explanations offered. The outrage softened into uncertainty.

Mira checked her inbox once more before bed.

No response yet.

She turned off her phone, crawled under her covers, and stared at the faint glow from the streetlight outside her window. Somewhere beyond the fence, beneath the soil, roots were working slowly, invisibly.

Nothing was wrong. Something was growing.

And she sensed—for the first time—that curiosity might require as much courage as ambition.

CHAPTER SEVEN

Roots and Wings

Growth is not always loud. Sometimes it arrives quietly, asking only whether you are paying attention.

The invitation did not arrive with spectacle. It arrived the way most meaningful things did in Mira's life—quietly, folded into the ordinary rhythm of an afternoon she would have otherwise forgotten.

The house was still. Delilah was at work, Professor Butterbean asleep in a sun-warmed square near the living room window. Mira sat at the kitchen table with her laptop open, the sleeves of her hoodie pushed up just enough to keep them clear of the counter. Early spring light filtered in through the window above the sink, pale but determined, catching on the edges of things rather than filling the room all at once.

Outside, the tulips were in their uneven moment. Some had opened just enough to offer their color, others still cupped and cautious, as though they were negotiating with the season. Mira liked them this way. It felt honest. Not everything had to bloom at the same time.

She reread the email she had finally answered the Wednesday night before.

Community Garden Recognition — Inquiry

It was still strange to see the words in her inbox. No logos. No congratulatory language. Just a request for clarification, for context, for history. Questions about how the East Birch Community Garden came to be what it was, how long she had been involved, who benefited, who helped. She had answered carefully, resisting the urge to downplay the work or dress it up. She explained that she hadn't planned the garden. She had found it abandoned years ago and started tending it because it bothered her to see good soil wasted. She wrote about seasons that failed and seasons that surprised her. She wrote about neighbors who stopped by without asking for credit. She wrote about food shared without cameras.

She had pressed send and gone to bed, assuming that would be the end of it.

Her phone rang the next afternoon.

Mira stared at it longer than she meant to, her pulse quickening in a way that didn't feel like fear so much as disorientation. She answered on the third ring.

"Hello?"

The voice on the other end belonged to a woman who spoke gently, as though she had learned long ago that urgency rarely improved understanding. She introduced herself as part of a regional civic foundation that supported community stewardship initiatives, particularly those led by young people.

“We don’t usually follow up this quickly,” the woman said, almost apologetically. “But your response was clear, and we wanted to speak with you directly.”

Mira listened, fingers curled loosely around the edge of the table.

The woman explained that the foundation had selected the East Birch Community Garden for a small community stewardship award. Not for innovation. Not for reach. For consistency. For longevity. For the way it had quietly become a reliable source of food and connection over time.

“There will be a brief ceremony in twelve days,” she said. “Nothing elaborate. We’d like you to attend, if you’re willing.”

Mira swallowed. “I didn’t apply,” she said, not defensively—just factually.

“We know,” the woman replied. “That’s part of why we’re calling.”

When the call ended, Mira remained where she was, phone resting against her palm, the room unchanged around her. The clock ticked. The heater clicked on and off. Outside, a breeze nudged the tulips, and one open bloom tilted toward the window as if listening.

The moment did not feel unreal. It felt oddly heavy, like something that belonged to a future version of her life had arrived early and was waiting for instructions.

She stood, went to the sink, and washed her hands. Warm water. Lemon soap. The familiar routine grounded her, pulling her back into her body.

When Delilah came home that evening, Mira told her quietly, standing in the kitchen doorway as her mother set her bag down.

Delilah listened without interrupting, her expression shifting slowly from curiosity to understanding. When Mira finished, Delilah reached out and pulled her into a hug that lingered longer than usual.

"I'm proud of you," she said.

Mira nodded against her shoulder. "I didn't do it for this."

"I know," Delilah said. "That's why it found you."

They didn't celebrate. They didn't post. They didn't tell anyone else.

The night went on as it always did—dinner, dishes, quiet television, Professor Butterbean claiming his place between them on the couch.

Outside, the tulips continued their slow negotiation with spring, opening only as much as they were ready to give.

The next twelve days passed without ceremony, but they did not pass unnoticed. School continued as it always did—bells, deadlines, crowded hallways—but something restless threaded through it all, tightening day by day.

Mira felt it most in the spaces between things. In the pauses before class started. In the way students hovered in doorways longer than necessary, phones already lifted, expressions half-curated before anything had even happened. Kindness challenges had not disappeared; they had multiplied, mutated, become competitive. What began as helping had turned into proof. Proof that you were generous. Proof that you were worthy of attention. Proof that you were doing life correctly.

Near the lockers one morning, a group of students clustered around a phone, replaying a clip again and again. A girl in the video handed a bag of groceries to a stranger, tears already prepared, voice trembling on cue.

"That one didn't hit," someone muttered. "She should've used the other audio."

"No, it was the timing," another said. "You gotta post right before lunch."

Mira waited for them to clear so she could open her locker. When they finally moved, she stepped into the space they left behind, the floor still sticky from a spilled drink no one had bothered to clean.

In class, teachers tried to redirect attention, but even lessons felt thinner lately. Half the room watched lectures through screens reflected in their glasses. Hands went up not with questions, but with stories about what had gone viral overnight. A substitute paused mid-sentence when a ring light slid out of a backpack and clattered onto the floor.

During lunch, Mira ate outside when she could. She liked the quiet behind the science wing, where the raised beds sat in tidy rows waiting for warmth. She brushed away dead leaves, pressed her fingers into the soil to check moisture, and made notes in her head about what would need to happen next. Early spring was about restraint. Nothing looked impressive yet, and that felt right.

Across the courtyard, voices carried.

"It doesn't even make sense," someone complained loudly. "I did the sandwich thing three times and nobody reposted it."

"I literally helped a stranger for free," another snapped. "That should count for something."

Mira didn't turn around. She focused on tightening a loose tie on the trellis. The words followed her anyway, sharp with disappointment, edged with accusation.

Count with whom, she wondered.

She passed Eli in the hallway later that afternoon. He moved carefully but efficiently, adjusting his backpack strap as he went, eyes fixed ahead. No one stopped him. No one filmed him. A few lockers down, Alina sat on the floor with her yarn looped neatly over her fingers, crocheting without urgency while she waited for class to start. A girl stepped over her without apology, camera trained on her own reflection instead.

Mira noticed these things without naming them. She noticed who showed up early. Who stayed late. Who fixed what broke and never said so. She noticed how the loudest efforts burned out fastest, while the quiet ones kept accumulating, unnoticed but intact.

At home, nothing changed. Delilah worked long shifts and came home tired but present. Mira cooked meals that stretched what they had without feeling thin. Professor Butterbean rotated his preferred chairs depending on the light. Life stayed grounded, ordinary in a way that felt increasingly rare.

Elsewhere, a small irritation sparked.

In the school office, a parent assigned by the city to unlock a reception hall for a last-minute civic event complained openly while waiting for paperwork.

"We're missing our own thing for this," she said into her phone. "Some kid's getting honored. I don't even know who."

A secretary glanced up. Another parent listened.

By the next morning, a name had surfaced.

Mira Howard.

No context. No explanation.

Just a question passed from mouth to mouth, gathering weight as it went.

Who?

By the following Monday, the rumors had hardened into assumptions.

They moved faster now, sharpened by repetition. Mira heard her name in fragments she wasn't meant to catch, felt conversations stall when she entered a room, noticed the way glances lingered a beat too long before sliding away. No one asked her directly. It was easier to build a story without her in it.

"Probably applied a bunch of times," someone said behind her in line for lunch.

"Or knew somebody," another voice added. "That's usually how it works."

A girl Mira barely recognized scoffed. "I don't buy the whole 'quiet saint' thing. Nobody gets picked just for being nice."

Mira took her tray and moved on. The comments followed her like background noise—present, irritating, but not something she could swat away. She didn't feel angry so much as confused. The version of her people were discussing didn't resemble the one who still had dirt under her nails and compost notes scribbled in the margins of her planner.

Social media circled but never landed. A few posts speculated about the award, tagging the city account, demanding transparency. Someone stitched together a video listing all the things that *should* count as community impact, complete with dramatic captions and a soundtrack that made indignation sound heroic. Mira watched none of it.

She had work to do.

Late winter still governed the garden, both at school and at East Birch. Beds rested under their coverings, soil dark and damp, holding its heat carefully. Mira spent her afternoons checking what little could be checked—tightening a hinge here, replacing a weathered label there. She knelt to clear debris from around emerging crowns, careful not to disturb what hadn't yet decided to surface.

The gate swung smoothly when she pushed it open, repaired sometime recently. She noticed the new bolts, the way the latch caught cleanly now instead of sticking. She didn't know who had fixed it, but she knew it hadn't been done for show. No note. No announcement. Just quiet attention.

She thought about that as she worked.

People kept mistaking visibility for value. They believed that if something mattered, it would announce itself. That effort was only real if it was seen. But gardens didn't work that way. Seeds split underground, out of sight. Roots reached before anything green appeared. If you rushed that process, you didn't get faster growth—you got rot.

Mira packed up her tools as the light faded, breath clouding briefly in the cooling air. The beds looked unchanged. Anyone passing by would have assumed nothing was happening.

That was fine.

At home, she spread her jacket over the back of a chair and sank into the quiet. Delilah was working late. Professor Butterbean claimed the warmest spot on the couch and watched her with half-lidded eyes.

Mira moved through her evening routine without hurry, letting the day settle.

She knew the ceremony was coming this Friday. She knew her name would eventually be spoken aloud in a room full of people who had never seen her work firsthand. The thought made her uneasy, but not enough to regret it. What had already grown could withstand a little attention.

Outside, the tulips held steady. Some blooms opened wider now, petals catching the last light. Others remained closed, conserving energy, unbothered by the progress around them.

Mira stood at the window for a moment before turning away.

What followed next would come when it was ready. For now, the roots held.

CHAPTER EIGHT

When Praise Feels Like Theft

When recognition no longer makes sense to the crowd, unrest is never far behind.

The first sign that something had shifted wasn't outrage.

It was confusion.

Mira felt it in the way conversations stalled when she walked past, in the way her name hovered at the edges of sentences without ever being spoken directly to her. Everyone at Northside Middle knew *something* had happened. What they didn't know was why it felt like a personal insult.

The announcement came during Wednesday morning advisories, delivered with the same neutral cadence used for schedule changes and weather delays.

"Please note," the assistant principal said over the intercom, "that the East Birch Community Stewardship Award ceremony will take place this Friday evening. Students receiving recognition will be excused early from last period."

A pause.

"And congratulations to Mira Howard for being selected this year."

The bell rang immediately after, slicing the moment cleanly in half.

For one suspended second, the hallway stayed eerily quiet. Then the sound came back in a rush—voices overlapping, lockers slamming harder than necessary, shoes scuffing against tile as people stopped walking and started talking.

"Who?!"

"Did she say Mira Howard?"

"That girl?"

Phones appeared almost instantly.

By second period, Mira's name had traveled the building faster than any official explanation could follow. Screens filled with searches that led nowhere useful. Her social media offered no clarity—no strategy, no polished brand, no trail of effort designed for consumption.

"That's it?" a girl scoffed loudly near the lockers. "She doesn't even try."

The phrase spread like a verdict.

She doesn't even try.

Mira heard it in passing at first. Twice before lunch, murmured just loudly enough to be shared. Again in the cafeteria line, spoken with the same sharp disbelief people used when accusing someone of cheating on a test.

She sat with Jaya at their usual table, her tray untouched, the noise of the room pressing in from every direction. The cafeteria had always been loud, but now it felt charged—voices overlapping, phones out, eyes darting as though everyone were waiting for the next rule to be announced.

"This doesn't make sense," a boy at the next table said, loud enough that he clearly wanted to be overheard. "There are people who actually do things. Like, all the time."

"I've been doing kindness challenges for months," someone else added, tapping their phone for emphasis. "I document everything. I literally have folders."

"Exactly," another voice chimed in, scoffing. "And she just… gardens?"

The word landed wrong, flattened into something small and unserious. Mira felt Jaya stiffen beside her.

Jaya opened her mouth, then closed it again, choosing Mira instead. "They act like effort only exists if it's archived," she muttered.

Mira nodded, though her chest felt tight. It wasn't the criticism that hurt most. It was the certainty with which they dismissed work they had never seen, never understood, simply because it hadn't been performed for them.

Mira stared at the table, hands folded in her lap. She didn't feel angry. She felt exposed, as if something private had been lifted out of context and held up for inspection.

Jaya leaned close. "You okay?"

"I didn't know it would feel like this," Mira admitted.

Neither had Delilah anticipated how quickly curiosity would curdle into something sharper.

That night, Delilah stood at the stove longer than necessary, stirring a pot that had already reached the right temperature. The motion was slow, absent-minded, the kind she fell into when she was thinking carefully about something she didn't want to say wrong.

"When people believe success is something you take," Delilah said at last, eyes still on the pot, "they can't imagine it being something that grows. They assume there's a trick. A shortcut. Someone being cheated out of what should've been theirs."

"I didn't take anything," Mira said quietly, not defensive, just stating the truth she knew.

Delilah turned then, resting the spoon against the rim. "I know," she said. "But they don't. And people get reckless when they feel embarrassed by that."

She reached for Mira's hand and squeezed it once, firm and grounding. "You didn't do anything wrong. That doesn't always protect you, but it matters."

By the following afternoon, confusion hardened into resentment.

A post appeared questioning the legitimacy of the award. Another accused the city of favoritism. Someone stitched together clips of trending kindness videos, arguing that *this* was what real impact looked like. Comments filled with certainty, with anger, with entitlement.

What unsettled Mira wasn't the criticism. It was the way people talked about compassion like it was currency.

"If it doesn't get seen, it doesn't count."

"If nobody knows you did it, what's the point?"

"She's gaming the system somehow."

She wasn't.

But logic had stopped mattering.

Within hours, the tension finally snapped.

It started in the main hallway just after sixth period. A group had gathered near the trophy case, phones already recording, voices raised not in argument but performance. Someone shouted that the award was a scam. Someone else yelled Mira's name like it was a challenge.

She wasn't there.

That didn't slow anything down.

A boy—red-faced, shaking—stepped forward and kicked the display case hard enough to rattle the glass. It didn't shatter, but the sound cracked through the hallway. Students screamed. Someone laughed nervously. Someone else cheered.

"THIS IS BULL—" the boy yelled before a teacher grabbed his arm.

Within minutes, administrators flooded the hall. The crowd swelled instead of dispersing, phones lifted higher now, capturing every second. Someone pushed. Someone else fell creating a small *almost* stampede.

Security was called.

Then the police.

The building went into lockdown—not because of a threat, but because no one could stop filming long enough to listen.

Mira sat in her classroom with the lights dimmed, heart hammering against her ribs. She could hear voices through the walls, the distant echo of authority trying to regain control.

She thought, not for the first time, about how quickly things unraveled when people felt denied something they believed they were owed.

By the official end of the day, one student was suspended indefinitely. Another was escorted out by an officer, face buried in his hoodie. Several videos were taken down. Others spread faster.

That night, Mira stood at her bedroom window longer than she usually did, watching the tulips sway gently in the cooling air. They were fully open now, unapologetically magenta against the darkening yard, their stems steady, their petals catching what little light remained.

They didn't explain themselves. They didn't justify their timing or apologize for the space they occupied. They bloomed because that was what came next.

Mira rested her forehead briefly against the glass.

Tomorrow might bring anything—questions, anger, judgment—she would walk inside anyway. She would stand where she was asked to stand and accept what had been offered, not because she wanted attention, but because refusing it wouldn't undo the work that had already been done.

She hadn't stolen anything.

She had simply grown something.

And growth, she was learning, had a way of revealing who was prepared for it—and who wasn't.

The next morning, the halls felt different—quieter, but not calmer. The noise had retreated into corners, leaving behind something brittle and tense. Teachers spoke more deliberately, choosing their words with care. Announcements reminded students about conduct and consequences, about respect and safety, without ever naming what had triggered them.

No one mentioned the award.

That absence felt louder than any announcement.

Mira went to class anyway. She took her seat, opened her notebook, and followed along as if the day were ordinary. A few students glanced at her and then quickly away. Others watched too long, curiosity tangled with resentment. She did not address it. She focused on the work in front of her, anchoring herself to what could be done rather than what could be said.

At the community garden that afternoon, the air felt steady again. The beds rested under their coverings. The gate held firm. Someone had repaired the compost bin latch overnight.

Eli worked at the far end of the space, focused on reinforcing a loose board. He nodded once when he saw her and went back to his task. Alina's crocheted squares fluttered softly along the fence, bright against the gray sky.

No one argued there.

The garden did not care who was trending. The soil held. The beds waited. Whatever anger had ignited elsewhere did not follow her past the gate.

Mira returned home to a house that felt unusually quiet. Delilah had laid her clothes out on the chair in Mira's room without saying anything—simple, thoughtful choices, nothing that tried too hard. A folded note rested on top, handwritten, short.

You don't need armor. Just be yourself.

Mira stood there for a long moment, fingers brushing the fabric. Outside her window, the tulips caught her eye, steady and open, as if they had already made their peace with being seen.

Down the street, a car passed too slowly. Somewhere, voices carried—excited, sharp, restless. Mira could feel it now, the pressure building, the sense that this evening would not stay contained inside a room with folding chairs and polite applause.

She washed her hands, grounding herself in the familiar ritual. Warm water. Soap. Breath.

Noise and judgment might fill the hall that evening, but she would arrive clean, steady, and unchanged.

She stepped away from the window, unaware of how many people were already planning to show up for a ceremony they didn't understand, furious about rules they had never learned.

CHAPTER NINE

The Ceremony

Noise always arrives early. Meaning shows up anyway.

The parking lot was already half full.

That alone told Mira something was off. Civic events at this center usually filled slowly—people arriving in polite waves, clustering near the doors, checking programs before committing to the evening. Tonight, cars lined the edges at odd angles, engines idling longer than necessary. Headlights swept across faces that weren't smiling.

Delilah eased into a space near the far row and cut the engine. For a moment, neither of them moved. Through the windshield, Mira could see handmade signs rising and falling near the entrance, cardboard edges bent from tight grips. Some were neatly lettered, others jagged, words crowded together as if written in a hurry. A few phones were already lifted, lenses pointed not at the building, but at the people arriving.

Delilah exhaled softly. "Storms don't ask permission," she said, not looking away from the scene. "They just show you what was already loose."

Mira glanced at her. Delilah's hands rested calmly in her lap, fingers relaxed. She wasn't bracing. She was steady.

"They're angry," Mira said.

"Yes," Delilah replied. "But not because of you." She turned then, meeting Mira's eyes. "People get loud when they've mistaken noise for power. When something quiet reminds them they misunderstood the lesson."

A shout rose near the doors—indistinct, more frustration than threat—but it was enough to make Mira's shoulders tense. Delilah noticed and reached over, pressing her palm briefly against Mira's arm.

"You remember what we talked about," she said gently. "You don't chase approval, and you don't argue with storms. You walk through them."

Mira nodded. She did remember. Delilah had learned that posture years ago, in circumstances far heavier than this. The lesson had been passed down without fanfare—how to stand when people misread your life, how to keep your footing when outrage looked for somewhere to land.

Outside, a group gathered tighter near the entrance. Someone laughed too loudly. Someone else shouted a question that wasn't meant to be answered. The chaos felt oddly disproportionate, as if the reaction had been waiting for any excuse to erupt.

"All this," Mira said quietly, gesturing toward the crowd, "because I didn't try to be seen."

Delilah's mouth curved, not quite a smile. "That's usually the part they can't forgive."

A car door closed nearby. Mira recognized Jaya's laugh—bright, a little forced—as she crossed the lot. Ms. Dollard followed more slowly, coat buttoned to her chin, posture upright, eyes alert but unafraid. When she spotted Mira, she lifted a hand and nodded once, a small, anchoring gesture.

Delilah opened her door. "No matter what unfolds out here," she said, voice low and sure, "remember this isn't a trial. It's a witness."

Mira stepped out into the cool air. The sounds sharpened immediately—voices overlapping, signs rustling, the faint wail of sirens somewhere farther down the road. She felt the weight of attention turn toward her, curious and accusatory all at once.

She squared her shoulders, not in defiance, but in readiness.

If society had lost its footing over a quiet girl and an honest garden, that wasn't hers to fix tonight.

She started toward the doors anyway.

The doors closed behind them with a soft, deliberate sound that felt almost ceremonial.

The noise didn't vanish entirely, but it dulled instantly, like a storm sealed behind glass. Inside the civic center, the air was warm and evenly lit, the kind of light that didn't demand attention. Voices lowered without being asked. Footsteps softened against polished floors. The chaos outside felt suddenly distant, unreal, as if it belonged to a different version of the world.

A woman with a simple name badge—**Elaine, Program Coordinator**—met them just inside the entrance. She smiled with practiced calm, the kind that came from repetition rather than denial.

"Mira Howard?" she asked gently.

Mira nodded.

Elaine's smile deepened. "We're glad you're here. Please—this way."

Two security officers stood nearby, unobtrusive but unmistakably present. They didn't posture. They didn't watch the guests so much as the doors.

"I'm sorry about the noise outside," Elaine said as they walked. "We've… learned to plan for it."

Delilah glanced at her. "This happens often?"

Elaine hesitated only a fraction of a second. "More than it used to. We've started hiring security routinely now—for ceremonies like this. Across the country."

Mira felt her steps slow.

"It's not personal," Elaine continued, lowering her voice. "It's cultural. People aren't angry at the recipients, really. They're angry at the idea that recognition can still exist without popularity attached to it. That something meaningful might not be measurable by reach."

Ms. Dollard hummed softly beside them. "That would be unsettling," she said, "for people who've invested everything in being seen."

Elaine nodded. "Exactly. When an award doesn't align with what they've been taught to value, it feels like an accusation."

They passed a table draped in linen where programs were stacked neatly, the paper thick, the font understated. No sponsor logos. No branding. Just names, dates, intentions.

Inside the main hall, rows of chairs were arranged with care, spaced just enough to feel generous rather than sparse. Soft music played—not something trending, but something patient, almost timeless. Conversations happened in low tones. People greeted one another with eye contact instead of phones.

Mira felt her shoulders loosen.

It was startling, the contrast. Outside, people clamored to be seen. Inside, no one seemed worried about disappearing.

“This,” Elaine said quietly, gesturing around them, “is what we’re trying to protect. A space where work can be honored without spectacle. Where effort doesn’t have to perform to be believed.”

Mira swallowed.

Delilah squeezed her hand once, pride steady and unshowy.

For a moment, the world felt aligned. As if this—this calm, this restraint, this reverence for things done well and quietly—was still possible. As if it could still be chosen.

Outside, a muffled chant rose and fell.

Inside, someone laughed softly.

The doors remained closed. And for now, that was enough.

Elaine guided them toward a long table set just beyond the main hall, tucked beneath warm lights that softened the edges of the room. The spread looked deliberate, generous—sliced pears and strawberries arranged in shallow bowls, clusters of grapes still cool from refrigeration, wedges of soft cheese paired with crackers stacked neatly instead of piled high. A glass dispenser of citrus punch caught the light, floating orange and lemon wheels like something meant to be noticed slowly.

"We know people had to rush here," Elaine said, setting down a stack of programs. "It felt right to feed them." She smiled, then excused herself, already being pulled gently toward another arrival.

Ms. Dollard reached for a napkin and surveyed the table with appreciation. "This is thoughtful," she said. "The kind of thoughtfulness that doesn't announce itself."

Delilah poured punch into small cups, handing one to Mira before taking her own. "It's hospitality," she said. "You can tell when it's offered freely."

Jaya hovered near the fruit, quiet for once. When she finally spoke, her voice was low. "I can't believe how angry they are," she said. "I mean… I've seen people mad online. But that?" She nodded toward the doors. "That's different."

Mira nodded. The unease she'd been holding finally had language. "They're not even mad at me," she said. "They're mad that it didn't work. All the posting. All the planning. They were promised something."

Jaya's mouth tightened. "Popularity," she said. "That's the promise. If you're visible enough, you're good enough. If people like you, you must be doing something right."

Ms. Dollard listened, fingers resting lightly on the edge of the table. "And if you're not?" she asked.

"Then you're suspect," Jaya replied. "Or you cheated. Or someone messed up the rules."

Mira looked around the room—the quiet conversations, the way people stood without angling for attention, the absence of phones held aloft. "It feels like they've replaced ethics with metrics," she said slowly. "Like being a good person isn't required anymore. Being popular is."

Delilah's expression softened, then steadied. "That shift didn't start with you," she said. "And it won't end tonight."

"But it feels… dangerous," Jaya said, surprising herself with the word. "Like if you don't perform the right way, people don't just ignore you. They come after you."

The thought settled heavily between them.

Ms. Dollard broke it gently. "Every era decides what it will reward," she said. "And every era punishes what reminds it of a better standard."

Mira swallowed. She hadn't expected this—hadn't imagined that being honest, being consistent, being uninterested in spectacle could feel like stepping into a moral crossfire. "I didn't plan for this," she said.

Delilah reached for her hand. "Integrity rarely comes with a warning label," she said. "But it does ask something of you."

Across the room, a hush began to form—not forced, not announced. Chairs shifted. Conversations softened. Someone adjusted the microphone.

Elaine stepped onto the small stage, calm and unhurried.

Mira took one more sip of punch, the citrus bright and grounding. Outside, the noise still pressed against the building, restless and unresolved. Inside, the room held.

Lines had been crossed and illusions shattered, but this space—this moment—remained intact.

Mira straightened, her heart steadying.

The ceremony was about to begin.

Elaine spoke first, her voice clear without being loud, the kind of voice that did not compete with a room but gathered it.

She welcomed everyone and thanked them for coming, yes—but she did not rush past the moment. She let it settle. She looked out at the audience, not scanning for cameras or reactions, but meeting faces as if each one mattered.

"We live in a loud world," she began, hands resting lightly on the podium. "A world that tells us—constantly—that if something matters, it must announce itself. That if effort is real, it will be visible. That goodness, to be valid, must be witnessed."

A few heads nodded. Mira felt the room lean in.

"But that story," Elaine continued, "has never been true for the things that actually hold us together."

She spoke then about stewardship—not as a title, not as an achievement, but as a posture. About showing up when no one is watching. About choosing care over credit. About tending work that may never trend, may never be rewarded, but nonetheless feeds people, shelters people, steadies people.

"Authentic effort accumulates the way roots do," she said. "Quietly. Invisibly. Patiently. And by the time it breaks the surface, it looks sudden to those who weren't paying attention."

There was a murmur of recognition—not applause yet, but something deeper.

Elaine's gaze softened. "Many of the people we honor tonight have been told, in one way or another, that they are doing it wrong. That they should be louder. Faster. More strategic. More visible. And yet, here they are—not because they played the game better, but because they chose not to replace integrity with performance."

She paused, allowing the words to stand on their own.

"If you've ever felt out of place in this culture," she said gently, "if you've wondered whether there's still room in the world for work done honestly and quietly, let tonight be an answer. You are not behind. You are not invisible. And you are not alone."

The applause that followed was not immediate. It arrived a second later—fuller, warmer, less polite. People clapped not to be seen doing so, but because something inside them had been named.

The first awardee was announced. Then the second. Each stood, walked to the stage, accepted a small plaque with a smile that looked more surprised than triumphant. The room remained calm, attentive, respectful.

Until it didn't.

It started as a sound rather than a sentence—a scoff that cut too sharply through the applause to be accidental.

"Lame!" a voice said from the left side of the room.

Heads turned.

A man stood halfway from his seat, face flushed, phone already lifted as if muscle memory had taken over. He didn't look embarrassed. He looked injured.

"This is unbelievable," he said, louder now. "My wife and I have spent thousands. Coaches. Consultants. Workshops since elementary school." He laughed once, sharp and humorless. "We did everything we were told."

A ripple of discomfort moved through the room.

Security shifted closer, but the man pressed on, words tumbling faster, less controlled.

"My kid's been documenting kindness for years," he continued. "Years. We just hit five hundred thousand subscribers last month. Do you know how hard that is?" He gestured wildly toward the stage. "And *this* is who you're honoring? People nobody's heard of?"

Someone gasped softly. Someone else shook their head.

"This is a joke," the man said, voice cracking now, anger fraying into something raw. "You're telling an entire generation that effort doesn't matter unless you pretend it didn't cost you anything. That you don't even have to try."

A security officer placed a steady hand on his arm. “Sir,” he said quietly.

The man pulled back, emboldened by the phones now pointed at him instead. “No—let them hear this. We played the game. We followed the rules. We invested. And now you’re changing the scoreboard because it makes you feel noble?”

Mira felt Jaya stiffen beside her. Ms. Dollard’s lips pressed into a thin line—not with anger, but with grief.

“Who are these people?” the man demanded, sweeping his arm across the stage. “Nobodies. You’re rewarding nobodies.”

The room stayed silent.

That seemed to unnerve him more than any argument could have.

Security moved decisively then, guiding him toward the aisle. He continued speaking as he was escorted out, voice echoing back toward the room.

“My kid deserves this. We earned this.”

The doors closed behind him with a final, solid sound.

Elaine returned to the microphone after only a brief pause. She did not apologize. She did not explain.

“Thank you for your patience,” she said simply. “We’ll continue.”

And they did.

Mira exhaled slowly, realizing she had been holding her breath. Her hands were steady in her lap. Her heart was not racing. What surprised her most was not the interruption—but how little it shook her.

She understood something then, with a clarity that settled deep rather than sharp.

The people shouting didn’t believe they were enough.

Not without proof. Not without numbers. Not without applause.

The people in this room already knew.

When Mira’s name was finally read, the applause was warm but unshowy. She stood, walked forward, and accepted the plaque with a quiet thank-you that did not try to fill the space.

She did not look toward the doors.

She did not need to.

Tonight had answered a question she hadn’t known how to ask.

Loving yourself first—seeing your own worth before demanding it from others—wasn’t arrogance.

It was armor.

And it was earned.

CHAPTER TEN

Still, They Knew

When you know who you are, noise loses its authority.

The last award had been handed out, the final recipient reseated, and the room settled into a collective exhale.

Elaine returned to the podium once the applause had fully faded. She did not reference the interruption from earlier, did not gesture toward the doors or the tension that had briefly tested the room. Instead, she trusted what the audience already knew.

"Every person recognized tonight was not selected by accident," she said, voice calm and unforced. "Not because they were flawless. Not because they were invisible. But because they were anchored."

She spoke of stewardship not as a title, but as a posture. Of effort that doesn't perform. Of integrity that doesn't need witnesses. Of people who know themselves well enough to keep going even when no one is applauding—and just as importantly, when someone is angry.

"There is a particular strength that comes from self-knowledge," Elaine said. "When you know who you are, noise loses its authority. Approval doesn't inflate you. Criticism doesn't undo you."

She let the room sit with that.

"If you leave here tonight and choose to keep being yourself—honestly, consistently, without bargaining with the culture—you may never trend. But you will matter. And you will be seen by the people who are actually paying attention."

The applause that followed was not immediate. It came a breath later—full, grounded, unhurried.

Elaine thanked the honorees, the families, the volunteers. The lights softened. Chairs shifted. The ceremony closed the way it had opened—without spectacle, without hurry.

Near the exit, a small group gathered briefly—Mira holding her plaque, Jaya squeezed in close, Ms. Dollard standing straight and proud, Delilah's arm resting lightly around Mira's shoulders. Someone offered to take a photo.

"Just one," Delilah said, smiling.

They stood together, unposed. No filters. No retakes. Mira felt the weight of the plaque in her hands—solid, modest, real.

The camera clicked.

"That's enough," Ms. Dollard said warmly, and it was.

As they walked toward the doors, Mira glanced once at the stage. The chairs were already being straightened. Programs collected. The room returning to what it was meant to be used for next.

By the time they stepped back outside, the chaos had thinned itself out.

The parking lot bore quiet evidence that a crowd had once been there—handwritten signs abandoned near a trash can, a crumpled poster taped crookedly to a light pole, a scattering of plastic cups pushed to the edges of the pavement. It felt careless. Telling.

A few officers still stood near the entrance, relaxed now, hands resting easily at their sides. Their presence was steady rather than imposing, and it seemed to give everyone permission to exhale.

People lingered in small clusters. Some took selfies beneath the civic center sign. A few parents chatted near open car doors, voices light again, the evening reclaiming its ordinary rhythm.

Mira paused as Ms. Dollard buttoned her coat.

"Thank you for coming," Mira said.

Ms. Dollard smiled, warmth undimmed. "I wouldn't have missed it for anything," she said. "Though it is well past my bedtime."

They laughed softly. Ms. Dollard gave Mira a brief, firm hug, then made her way carefully to her car.

Jaya piled into the back seat of Delilah's sedan as Mira climbed into the front. Delilah pulled out slowly, the headlights catching the last of the discarded signs before the lot gave way to the road.

They passed the civic center, then the turnoff, then the quiet stretch leading toward the highway.

The night widened ahead of them.

Jaya leaned back in the rear seat, exhaling for what felt like the first time all night.

"Okay," Jaya said finally. "That man was… unhinged."

Mira let out a small laugh. "That feels accurate."

"I recognized him," Jaya added. "He's the dad of the kid who got suspended yesterday. The one who kicked the trophy case."

Delilah nodded once, unsurprised. "Anger that's practiced tends to be inherited."

"What got me," Jaya said, quieter now, "is how nobody reacted. Like—really reacted. No shouting back. No clapping. Nothing."

Mira had noticed that too. "It was like… the room didn't accept his version of reality."

Delilah glanced at Jaya in the rearview mirror. "Because it didn't belong there," she said. "Everyone in that room already knew who they were. People like that"—she didn't need to name him—"they need resistance to feel real. When they don't get it, they unravel."

Jaya laughed softly, then grew thoughtful. "So they weren't picked by accident," she said. "Any of them."

"No," Delilah replied. "They were picked because they're steady. Because they've done the work of knowing themselves."

They rode in silence for a moment, the road humming beneath the tires, the highway lights passing in a steady rhythm.

Delilah broke it gently. "Can I tell you something?" she asked, eyes still on the road.

Mira turned toward her. Jaya sat up a little straighter.

"There was a time," Delilah began, "when I thought being overlooked meant I had failed. I was younger than you are now, Mira, and I believed very sincerely that if people didn't notice my effort, it meant it hadn't counted."

She paused at a red light, fingers tightening briefly on the steering wheel.

"I worked for a woman once who thrived on attention," she continued. "Everything she did was visible. Strategic. Praised. And I watched her rise quickly—faster than anyone else in the office. Meanwhile, I stayed late, fixed problems no one wanted to claim, carried responsibility that never came with credit."

Jaya frowned. "That sounds… familiar."

Delilah smiled faintly. "At the time, it felt unbearable. I started questioning myself. Wondering if I needed to become louder. Sharper. More impressive. I almost did."

The light changed. The car moved forward.

"But something stopped me," Delilah said. "One afternoon, that same woman made a decision that looked brilliant on the surface and disastrous underneath. Everyone applauded it—right up until it collapsed. And when it did, all the quiet work I had done—the unglamorous work—was the only thing holding the place together."

Mira listened closely.

"No one thanked me," Delilah went on. "No apology. No acknowledgment. But something shifted in me. I realized that my worth had never been dependent on their recognition. I had known who I was all along. I had just been waiting for someone else to confirm it."

She exhaled softly. "That was the day I stopped waiting. I gave myself the nod."

She glanced briefly at Mira. "That night, I promised myself I would never again confuse visibility with value. And I would raise my child to know the difference."

The car grew quiet again, but it was a different kind of quiet now—full rather than empty.

"I didn't get braver all at once," Delilah said after a moment. "I got quieter. More settled. I stopped trying to prove myself to rooms that didn't understand me. And something unexpected happened."

Jaya leaned forward slightly. "What?"

"I started noticing who *was* paying attention," Delilah said. "Not the loudest people. The steady ones. The ones who showed up when things went wrong. They trusted me. They saw me. Opportunities came—not flashy ones—but lasting ones. And I realized I hadn't been invisible at all. I had just been standing in a different light."

Mira swallowed, emotion pressing unexpectedly behind her ribs.

"That man tonight," Delilah continued, voice steady but softer now, "he reminded me of who I almost became. Someone convinced that worth had to be wrestled from the world. Someone who believed the rules were rigged because he never learned how to listen for a different standard."

She shook her head once. "That kind of anger eats people from the inside. It convinces them that everyone else is the problem."

Jaya was quiet for a long moment. "So… when no one reacted," she said slowly, "that wasn't weakness."

Delilah smiled, just a little. "It was strength. Collective strength. Everyone in that room had already done the work of knowing themselves. His noise had nowhere to attach."

Mira looked down at the plaque again, tracing the edge with her thumb. "I didn't feel scared," she admitted. "I thought I would. But I didn't."

"That's how you know," Delilah said. "Fear feeds on uncertainty. When you know who you are, it starves."

They turned onto Jaya's street then, the houses familiar, porch lights glowing softly. Delilah slowed, pulling to the curb.

"Thank you," Jaya said as she gathered her things, voice sincere. "For tonight. For… letting me see that."

Mira smiled. "I'm glad you were there."

After Jaya closed the car door and disappeared up the walk, soon quickly flashing the sconce light to indicate she was safely inside, Delilah pulled away again. The road opened, empty and calm.

Mira rested her head lightly against the window, the plaque still warm in her hands. She thought about gardens, about roots forming long before anything broke the surface. About rooms that knew how to hold their ground.

Outside, somewhere else, a video was already spreading—raised voices, outrage sharpened for clicks.

Inside the car, Mira felt something steadier than pride. She felt known, and she knew herself.

PART III

ALIGNMENT

CHAPTER ELEVEN

The Video That Missed the Point

Noise spreads faster than truth—but truth has roots.

By Monday morning, the ceremony itself had already been flattened into a rumor.

Mira realized that before she even reached her locker.

The hallway felt normal on the surface—students rushing, shoes squeaking, someone calling out a name across the crowd—but under it there was a tension that made the air feel thinner. People were holding something. Waiting to release it.

A laugh burst out too sharply near the water fountain.

A phone screen flashed as someone turned it toward a friend.

A group near the trophy case leaned in close, faces lit by the glow of a video playing on repeat.

Mira didn't have to ask what it was. She could tell from the way eyes darted toward her and then away, as if looking too long might implicate them.

It wasn't footage of the awards. That detail alone told Mira everything she needed to know about what people were actually hungry for.

No one cared about the speeches, about the way names had been spoken carefully into a microphone, about the quiet gravity of people being thanked for work done without spectacle. No one cared about the quiet applause that had felt, to Mira, like something sacred.

The video that had caught fire was the heckler, isolated and enlarged until he became the entire event.

Someone had stitched together his outburst with shaky clips from the parking lot: cardboard signs bobbing near the doors, police lights flaring against the night, voices rising and collapsing into the same sentence over and over again. The edit wasn't accidental. It was engineered to feel like proof.

A caption slid across the screen in bold, dramatic font:

WHEN DO QUIET PEOPLE START STEALING OPPORTUNITIES?

In the comments, people didn't ask what had actually happened.

They chose a side.

Mira reached her locker and spun the dial with steady hands. A familiar laugh cut through the noise just to her left—high, performative.

Brennan Cole leaned against the lockers a few feet down, phone already in his hand, pretending not to watch her while very clearly watching her. He was popular in the way algorithms rewarded—loud, reactive, constantly filming himself reacting to other people's moments.

Mira opened her locker and felt her stomach dip—not because of what was inside, but because of what was taped neatly to the door.

A printed screenshot of the video.

The same bold caption stretched across it:

WHEN DO QUIET PEOPLE START STEALING OPPORTUNITIES?

Under it, written in black marker, the words slanted and smug:

WHO IS MIRA HOWARD?

Brennan's laugh followed, casual, practiced. "Wild night, huh?" he said, not quite looking at her. "Guess anybody can win stuff now."

Mira said nothing. She peeled the paper off carefully, folded it once, then again, as if gentleness might strip it of power. She slid it into her pocket and closed her locker.

Brennan watched her go, his phone already lifted again, hunting for the next moment worth feeding the machine.

In first period, the teacher tried to keep things moving. Roll call. Warm-up. A reminder about the quiz.

But the room kept flickering.

A boy at the back replayed the video with the sound off, nodding along as if silence made it truer. Two girls whispered, giggling in that tight way people giggle when they're nervous but don't want to admit it.

Mira kept her eyes on the board.

Her pencil moved.

Her breathing stayed even.

She was not going to hand them the satisfaction of a reaction.

That was, she suspected, what the video wanted most.

At lunch, Jaya slid into the seat across from Mira and set her phone face-down like it was something contaminated. The gesture felt deliberate, almost ceremonial, as if refusing to let the device dictate the conversation.

"They think the video *is* the story," she said, voice low.

Mira stared at her tray. The food smelled fine. Her appetite was gone anyway. "It's easier," she said.

Easier to believe somebody had been robbed than to admit the rules they'd lived by were never real. Easier to side with anger than to sit with humility. Easier to call integrity suspicious than to face what performance had done to them.

Around them, the cafeteria buzzed with recycled outrage.

"You saw the dad, right?" someone said at the table behind them. "He was spitting facts."

"No, he was embarrassing," another voice replied, but even that sounded amused rather than concerned.

"I'm just saying," a boy insisted, louder, "my cousin's been in leadership workshops since third grade. If anybody deserves recognition, it's people who put in the work."

Jaya's jaw tightened. "They're still talking like recognition is a prize you win for proving you want it the most."

Mira nodded slowly. "And like goodness is a performance review."

A group at the far table had set up a phone on a lunch tray, filming a reaction video to the heckler's rant. They gestured dramatically, pausing to make faces for the camera, acting like they were breaking down an important cultural moment.

None of them mentioned the actual awardees.

None of them asked what the projects were.

The content wasn't about truth. It didn't even pretend to be.

It was about momentum—about who could ride the wave the longest without stopping to ask where it was actually going.

Mira's phone buzzed once. Then again.

Two unknown numbers.

A DM request from someone she didn't follow.

A comment under a months-old photo of her garden bed:

FRAUD.

Her fingers hovered over the screen.

She didn't respond.

She didn't delete it.

She simply turned the phone off.

Across the cafeteria, Alina sat near the wall, crocheting with the same steady rhythm she always had, her yarn looped over her fingers, catching briefly at her knuckle. No one asked about her work. No one teased her today either. Everyone was too busy chasing a bigger target.

Eli passed by the lunchroom entrance, crutches moving with quiet efficiency. He didn't look toward the noise. He moved as if he had learned, long ago, not to negotiate with people who needed chaos to feel alive.

Mira watched him for a brief moment and felt something settle.

There were still people like them—quiet, consistent, uninterested in proving anything to anyone watching from a distance.

People who didn't owe the world a performance, and knew it.

After school, Mira walked past the trophy case where the glass had been replaced from the incident earlier in the week. The new pane was too clean, too obvious, a reminder that consequences had already arrived once—and could arrive again.

Outside, the cool air carried the faint scent of thawing earth. The sun sat low, bright without warmth.

Mira didn't go straight home.

She went to the community garden.

It was still early spring there—preparation season. Beds covered. Soil resting. Strawberries waking slowly under mulch. The garden did not look like success to anyone who expected results to be immediate. It looked like patience.

Mira unlocked the gate and stepped inside.

The moment she did, her shoulders dropped, as if the air itself gave permission.

The hose was coiled neatly against the fence.

The trash bin lid, which had been loose last week, held firm now.

A board on the far trellis had been reinforced.

No note.

No credit.

Just work.

Mira knelt near one of the beds and brushed away dead leaves, exposing the dark soil beneath. Her fingers pressed into it gently, checking moisture. Not frozen. Not warm. Somewhere in between.

She stayed there until her thoughts stopped racing.

When she finally opened her email later that evening, a message sat at the top of her inbox.

No subject line.

No signature.

Just one sentence.

Saw the video…that's not the whole story.

Beneath it—almost as an afterthought—another line appeared.

Keep tending what matters.

Mira stared at the screen longer this time.

The phrasing was careful. Not defensive. Not curious. Certain.

It wasn't praise. It wasn't outrage. It wasn't advice.

It was recognition—quiet, unmarketable, real.

And whoever had written it knew more than they were saying.

Her heart lifted in a way that startled her, not because she needed approval, but because the message proved what she had started to suspect.

The loudest voices weren't the only ones.

There were watchers.

People who could still see beneath the noise.

People who understood that viral didn't mean valuable.

Mira closed her laptop and went to wash her hands, letting warm water run over her fingers until they felt like hers again.

Then she went back to her room and set the plaque on her dresser—not in a spotlight, not like a trophy, but like a marker.

A reminder.

The video had gone viral, spreading fast and loud, fed by outrage and repetition.

The ceremony hadn't, and that absence felt intentional—almost protective. And that told her everything.

CHAPTER TWELVE

The Weight of Being Seen

Integrity is tested most when it leaves familiar ground.

Delilah suggested the mall.

Not because they needed anything, but because it was neutral ground—public enough to be real, ordinary enough to test whether the world outside school had noticed what the internet was busy shouting.

Saturday afternoon traffic was thick but patient, the kind that suggested people had nowhere urgent to be. Mira watched the automatic doors slide open and closed as they approached, families spilling in and out, arms full of shopping bags, faces already tired before they'd even begun.

The warmth hit them first. Then sound.

Music layered over announcements. Laughter cutting through the hum. The low, constant roar of people moving without quite knowing why.

They started at Kate Spade.

Mira moved slowly through the store, taking in the careful order of it all—the way the bags were angled just so, the soft lighting designed to feel effortless. She lifted one from the display, feeling the weight of it, appreciating the craftsmanship without imagining it as hers.

A woman browsing nearby glanced at Mira, then looked again. Her eyes lingered for a second too long, not intrusive, just curious. Mira noticed and then let it pass.

Delilah smiled faintly. "Cute," she said. "Not in our budget."

Mira nodded. "That's okay."

Delilah studied her face. "You're sure?"

"Yeah," Mira said, meaning it. "I don't feel like I'm missing something."

Delilah leaned against the counter, thoughtful. "I spent a lot of years thinking money was proof," she said quietly. "That if I could afford what other people had, I'd finally feel settled."

Mira waited.

"It took me a long time to realize that peace doesn't come from matching someone else's life," Delilah continued. "It comes from wanting less—not because you're deprived, but because you're content."

They left the store empty-handed, unbothered.

The Apple Store was louder. Brighter. Tables crowded with hands swiping and tapping, faces tense with comparison. A teenager argued with a sales associate about storage capacity as if it were a moral issue. Mira watched for a moment, struck by how quickly frustration bloomed around things meant to make life easier.

Another glance—this time from a man waiting near the Genius Bar. Recognition flickered, then softened into something like uncertainty. He didn't say anything. Neither did she.

Delilah leaned close. "We're still on the same phone plan from three years ago," she whispered. "And somehow, the world hasn't ended."

Mira smiled. "It works."

"It does," Delilah agreed. "Most things do, if you don't demand they prove something."

They moved on, unhurried.

Near the game store, noise spilled into the hallway. A knot of adolescents crowded the entrance, voices loud, bodies careless. One boy shoved another playfully but too hard. A display rattled. A parent barked from a distance without moving closer.

Delilah stopped just long enough to take it in.

"You never acted like that," she said, not with pride but with quiet wonder. "You had energy. Curiosity. But you were never reckless with it."

Mira shrugged. "I don't like feeling out of control."

Delilah exhaled. "I've always felt lucky," she said softly. "But sometimes I think I was chosen. Trusted with you."

Mira felt that land. "I think that goes both ways."

At Barnes & Noble, time stretched.

Mira ran her fingers along spines, pulling books down to read first lines, then sliding them back into place. She lingered in the essays, drifted through fiction, paused too long in poetry. Delilah settled into a chair near the café, watching her with an ease that came from years of knowing she didn't need to be managed.

A woman passing by slowed, eyes flicking between Mira and a phone held loosely at her side. She smiled—small, approving—then kept walking.

Mira felt it again. The noticing.

Not admiration. Not spectacle.

Recognition.

They shared a Cinnabon next, tearing it apart instead of cutting it, cinnamon sugar sticking to their fingers. Delilah laughed as the icing dripped despite her efforts.

"This is our splurge," she said. "Worth every penny."

In a clothing store advertising end-of-season sales, racks overflowed with sweaters and hoodies marked down to make room for spring. Mira moved slowly, touching fabrics, letting herself choose without urgency.

She pulled a golden yellow hoodie from the rack. Warm, earthy, slightly subdued, it presents as muted mustard, not bright yellow.

"I like this," she said.

Delilah checked the tag and nodded. "That's reasonable."

Mira slipped it on. In the mirror, she looked exactly like herself—comfortable, unremarkable, grounded.

Another glance from a shopper passing behind her. Curious. Familiar.

They bought it.

Hours passed that way. Four of them, nearly unnoticed. Browsing. Sitting. Watching people rush, argue, scroll, buy things they seemed unsure they wanted. Chaos worn like a uniform.

Mira felt separate, but not lonely. An outsider, but a peaceful one.

She didn't wish to be louder. Or cooler. Or more impressive.

She felt steady.

And as they finally turned toward the exit, the mall buzzing behind them like a contained storm, Mira understood something clearly:

This was what it looked like to be seen without performing.

To move through noise without becoming it.

To belong to yourself first.

They didn't stop at the food court so much as arrive there. Positioned near the corridor leading to the parking garage.

it was where the mall funneled everyone eventually—voices rising, trays clattering, the smell of sugar and grease hanging heavy in the air. Delilah ordered drinks while Mira scanned for an empty table, her new hoodie soft against her wrists.

That was when the noticing changed.

Not the quiet glances she'd felt all afternoon. This was different—sharp, electric, communal.

A boy near the soda machine froze mid-laugh, his eyes widening. He nudged the girl beside him, who followed his gaze, then whispered something urgently to the group clustered around her.

Phones came out.

Not all at once, but fast enough to feel coordinated.

"Wait—are you her?" a girl asked, stepping closer, phone already angled upward.

Mira felt Delilah's posture shift beside her. Protective. Alert.

"Hey," another voice chimed in, louder. "It *is* her. That's Mira Howard."

The name moved through the space like a spark.

A small semicircle formed—six, maybe eight kids, roughly Mira's age. Curious more than hostile, but close enough to feel invasive. Someone laughed nervously. Someone else started recording outright.

Delilah opened her mouth.

Mira reached out and touched her arm.

"It's okay," she said quietly.

Delilah hesitated, then let her daughter step forward.

"Yes," Mira said, her voice steady but gentle. "That's my name."

A boy in a varsity jacket scoffed. "So you just, like… garden?"

A couple of kids laughed.

Mira didn't flinch.

"I do," she said. "And other things."

"Then why'd you get the award?" another girl asked, not cruel, just blunt. "Some of us have been doing kindness challenges for years."

The phones tilted closer.

Mira took a breath. She felt her heartbeat, but it didn't race. It stayed with her.

"I don't really think of it as competing," she said. "Or proving something."

A boy rolled his eyes. "That's easy to say when you're winning."

Mira met his gaze. Not defensively. Honestly.

"I don't feel like I won anything," she said. "I just… kept showing up where I was needed."

That landed.

Not silence—this wasn't a movie—but a shift. The laughter thinned. Someone lowered their phone.

"Look," Mira continued, choosing her words carefully, "I think helping people matters. But I don't think it stops mattering if nobody sees it. And I don't think it matters *more* if everyone does."

A girl frowned. "So you don't care about credit?"

Mira shook her head. "I care about people."

Delilah watched, her expression unreadable now—not concern, but something like awe.

"I think when you start doing good things to be noticed," Mira said, "you end up needing the noticing more than the good thing itself. And that gets… loud."

No one laughed this time.

One of the boys cleared his throat. "So you're saying we're doing it wrong?"

"I'm saying it's not about right or wrong," Mira replied. "It's about why. If you help someone because it's right, that still counts—even if nobody posts it."

A phone clicked off.

Another kid stepped back, then another. The semicircle

loosened.

Someone muttered, "She's not what I expected."

Mira smiled, small and unbothered. "That's okay."

The group dispersed—not dramatically, just quietly, as if a spell had been broken. Conversations resumed. Trays were picked up. Attention moved on, looking for something louder.

Delilah let out a breath she hadn't realized she'd been holding.

"You didn't owe them anything," she said.

"I know," Mira replied. "But sometimes people are just… confused."

They found a table near the window. Outside, the parking lot shimmered with late afternoon light.

Delilah studied her daughter for a long moment, then smiled.

"I don't think they'll forget that," she said.

Mira shrugged, unbothered. "I hope they don't feel small," she said. "That wasn't the point."

Delilah reached across the table and squeezed her hand.

Around them, the food court buzzed back to life—chaotic, loud, endlessly hungry for the next moment.

But at their table, there was space.

Respect had done what spectacle couldn't.

They didn't leave the mall right away.

Delilah suggested walking a little more, not to buy anything, but to let the moment settle without rushing it into meaning. Mira welcomed that. Her chest still felt warm—not with adrenaline, but with something steadier, like a door that had closed cleanly instead of slamming.

They passed a store selling scented candles and home décor. Mira lingered, lifting lids, inhaling lavender, cedar, something faintly citrus. Ordinary comforts. The kind meant to slow people down. She noticed that her hands weren't shaking. Her voice hadn't cracked. She hadn't replayed her words yet, searching for mistakes.

That surprised her.

She had always assumed that speaking up—really speaking—would cost something. That it would require giving away a piece of herself or bracing for consequences she couldn't predict. But standing there in the food court, choosing honesty over performance, hadn't taken anything from her at all.

It had clarified her.

They sat for a while on a low bench near a planter, watching people pass. A couple argued quietly. A child tugged impatiently at his father's sleeve. Two girls compared shopping bags like trophies. Mira observed it all with a strange sense of distance—not detachment, but discernment.

"I didn't feel small," she said eventually.

Delilah turned toward her. "After?"

"During," Mira corrected. "I thought I might. But I didn't."

Delilah smiled. Not the proud smile she gave when Mira achieved something measurable, but the softer one she reserved for moments of becoming. "That's how you know you were standing on your own ground."

Mira nodded. She thought about the way the crowd had leaned in, hungry not for truth but for spectacle. And how quickly that hunger had faded when it wasn't fed.

"They weren't really mad at me," Mira said. "They were mad that it didn't work. The posting. The trying so hard."

"Yes," Delilah said. "And you didn't insult them by pretending otherwise."

They walked again, slower now. Mira felt the weight of the day—not heavy, just full. The mall's chaos no longer pressed in on her. It moved around her instead, like weather she knew how to dress for.

Near the exit, a woman passed them and smiled—a real smile, brief and unremarkable. Nothing about it asked to be remembered, yet Mira felt it land more deeply than any of the attention earlier.

Outside, the air was cooler. Late afternoon light stretched long shadows across the pavement. Mira pulled her new hoodie closer around herself, feeling its warmth.

As they reached the car, Delilah paused, keys in hand. "You know," she said, "a lot of people spend their whole lives trying to recover from the moment they first learned to perform instead of be honest."

Mira considered that. "I don't think I want to forget who I am just to be liked."

Delilah met her eyes. "You won't," she said. "You've already learned something most people don't learn until much later—if at all."

They drove home with the windows cracked, the quiet companionable rather than empty. Mira watched the city thin into neighborhoods, then into familiar streets. The day replayed in her mind—not as a series of judgments, but as a sequence of choices she felt at peace with.

When they pulled into the driveway, Mira stayed seated for a moment longer, hands resting in her lap.

Speaking up hadn't cost her anything.

It had given her something back.

Not applause. Grounding. A steadiness she hadn't expected.

As she stepped out of the car, Mira understood that what came next didn't require preparation. She already knew who she was. Present. Grounded. Unmistakably herself.

Today had proven that.

CHAPTER THIRTEEN

The Offer That Made Sense

Not every open door is an assignment.

By early May, the town had settled into a different kind of rhythm.

Spring was no longer tentative or polite. It had committed. The mornings arrived warm and generous, the air already thick with pollen and promise, and by midday the sun pressed down with a familiarity that hinted at the long Southern summer waiting just ahead. Nothing about it felt rushed. It felt earned.

The community garden mirrored that same confidence.

Mira moved through the beds just after sunrise, her steps unhurried, her hands steady. Leaves had grown broader. Stems had thickened. The work she'd done weeks earlier—when the soil was still cool, when nothing visible suggested success—now announced itself quietly in green abundance.

She knelt beside the tomatoes first, checking for splitting, adjusting ties where vines leaned too heavily on their supports. Pepper plants showed their first small blossoms, pale and hopeful. Strawberries hid low beneath their leaves, blushing red where the sun had found them. The herbs had come into themselves—basil lush and sweet, rosemary sturdy, mint unapologetically invasive.

Nothing felt dramatic.

Everything felt alive.

The gate opened smoothly. The hose bib turned without resistance. Random parts now clicked with a quiet finality that told her someone had cared enough to fix them properly. Along the fence, Alina's crocheted squares fluttered in the breeze—colorful, imperfect, softening the rigid geometry of metal and wire.

Mira harvested with discernment rather than excitement. Enough strawberries for Ms. Dollard. Enough herbs for the assisted living kitchen. Enough produce for the pantry box near the school counselor's office—the one that never needed an announcement.

And still, there was more.

By the time she and Delilah pulled into the farmers market lot, the car smelled like warm earth and green things. Basil and soil clung to the air, grounding and unmistakable.

White tents lined the pavement in clean rows, their canopies catching the early light. The market hummed gently—vendors setting out crates, coffee cups steaming in hands, a guitarist tuning strings without urgency. The smell of peaches mingled with fresh bread and something fried that made Mira's stomach stir.

Their table was simple. A folding table with a clean cloth. Baskets arranged thoughtfully rather than artfully. Strawberries portioned into small cartons. Herbs bundled with twine. A handful of early tomatoes, modest and not yet boastful.

Delilah set out the sign she'd written carefully the night before:

Community Garden Produce — Pay What You Can

People paused.

Some paid exactly what they could. Some paid more. A few simply nodded, took what they needed, and murmured thank you in a way that suggested the exchange mattered.

A woman in scrubs bought basil and asked how Mira kept it so fragrant.

"Sun," Mira said honestly. "Water. Time."

A little boy stared at the strawberries as though they were rare.

His mother hesitated, counting bills. Delilah pretended not to notice and slipped an extra carton into the bag.

"For the ride home," she said.

The woman's shoulders relaxed. She nodded once, understanding the gift without being made small by it.

Mira watched it all with the quiet steadiness she'd grown into.

No applause.

No spectacle.

Just impact, moving outward in small, faithful ways.

The email arrived on a normal afternoon that felt otherwise unremarkable.

Mira was in the kitchen, sleeves pushed up, working her way through a meal she knew by heart.

Salisbury steak—hand-shaped hamburger patties, pressed gently so they stayed tender—waited on a plate beside the stove. She had already browned them, lifting each one carefully, setting them aside while the pan still held the good parts: rendered fat, browned bits, the foundation of flavor Delilah had taught her never to waste.

The onions she chopped now would melt into that pan, turning soft and golden, thickening into a homemade brown gravy the way her grandmother once had, by sight rather than measurement. No packet. No shortcuts. Just patience, flour dusted in slowly, broth poured with intention, salt adjusted by taste.

On the back burner, golden Yukon potatoes simmered until their skins split easily under a fork. Mira mashed them by hand—no mixer—adding warm milk and butter a little at a time until the texture felt right. Delilah always said potatoes should feel like comfort before they ever reached the plate.

Green beans steamed nearby, seasoned simply with salt, pepper, garlic, onion and a small piece of ham that had been saved just for this purpose. It was an old habit—stretching flavor, honoring scarcity—that Delilah had learned from her own mother and passed down without ceremony.

Cooking in their house wasn't about recipes written down.

It was inheritance.

Each dish carried memory the way some families carried stories—lessons folded into repetition, wisdom transferred hand to hand. Mira had learned early that feeding people was a language of care, one that didn't require explanation.

Professor Butterbean lounged near the doorway, tail flicking lazily. The radio hummed low, something old and warm that Delilah liked to play while cooking.

Her phone vibrated against the counter.

Mira ignored it.

She finished the onion, slid it into the pan, and wiped her hands on a towel before glancing down. The screen lit up with a subject line that stopped her mid-motion.

Teen Kitchen Partnership — Inquiry for Mira Howard

Her heart didn't race.

It paused.

The sender wasn't someone she recognized, but the email address looked professional. Legitimate. Mira opened it slowly, as if speed might change what it said.

The message wasn't loud.

It didn't gush or flatter or pretend to know her personally. It introduced the company, explained its mission, and then—carefully—explained why they were reaching out to her.

They hadn't found her through trends or follower counts. They had noticed her through quieter channels: a community committee mention, a farmers market recommendation, a short local article that hadn't traveled far but had been written with care.

They were developing a cookware line for teens—durable, affordable, designed for hands still learning confidence in the kitchen. They weren't looking for someone who performed cooking. They were looking for someone who lived it.

They liked that Mira didn't stage her meals.

They liked that she cooked as an act of care rather than content.

They liked that she didn't seem interested in being impressive.

The offer was outlined plainly. A modest guaranteed payment. Commission tied to actual sales. Creative freedom. No scripts. No required posting schedule. No pressure to manufacture enthusiasm.

They asked—politely—if she would be open to a conversation.

Mira reread the email twice.

It made sense.

Which was exactly what unsettled her.

Delilah leaned in, reading over her shoulder, then straightened with a slow exhale. “Well,” she said softly. “That’s… something.”

Mira set the phone down as if it were warm.

They finished dinner in a quieter rhythm.

Then Delilah suggested the call.

“Just listen,” she said. “You don’t have to say yes.”

Mira agreed.

The next afternoon, they sat at the kitchen table with the window open, warm May air drifting in. Mira’s hands rested around a mug she wasn’t drinking from.

The brand representative introduced herself as Lena Ellis—calm voice, no rushing, no flattery.

“I want to start by saying we’ve done our homework,” Lena said. “Not in an invasive way. In a respectful way. We were trying to understand whether you align with what we’re building.”

Mira listened.

Lena spoke about teens being sold a version of cooking that was either performative or impossible—perfect kitchens, perfect bodies, perfect outcomes. She wanted something different: a line that made cooking feel accessible, grounding, human.

"We don't need you to be louder than you are," Lena said. "We need you to be exactly who you already are."

Delilah watched Mira carefully.

The offer was real.

The numbers weren't obscene, but they were meaningful.

Meaningful enough to solve a few problems.

Meaningful enough to create new ones.

When the call ended, Lena sent a packet with details and a timeline, and then—crucially—space.

"Take your time," she said. "If this is right, it will still be right in a week."

That night, the house was quiet in the way it only got when Delilah had finished cleaning and Mira had finished homework. The world outside hummed—

cars passing, distant music, someone laughing on a porch.

Mira sat on the top step of the back porch with Professor Butterbean beside her, warm and loyal.

Delilah joined her with two cups of tea, careful as she stepped onto the porch so the liquid wouldn't slosh over the rim.

The steam carried a familiar scent—citrus and mint layered with something softer underneath. It was Peach Tranquility and Citrus Mint, steeped together the way they always did when neither of them could decide. Delilah had added honey, just enough to round the edges without dulling the brightness. It was their quiet indulgence, small and dependable, the kind of preference you develop when life has taught you to notice what actually comforts you.

She handed one cup to Mira, their fingers brushing briefly. Mira wrapped both hands around it, letting the warmth settle into her palms before she took a sip. The taste was exactly what she expected—clean, floral, soothing in a way that felt almost intentional.

Delilah sat beside her, exhaling as if the tea itself had given permission to slow down.

They sat for a moment before speaking, the silence doing its own kind of thinking.

"We could use the money," Delilah said finally. She didn't sound ashamed of it. Just honest.

Mira nodded. "I know."

Delilah traced the rim of her cup with her thumb. "There are things I've learned to live without. But sometimes… I wonder what it would feel like not to have to measure everything."

Mira stared out at the yard. "What would they want from me?"

Delilah didn't pretend not to understand the question. "Time," she said. "Energy. Maybe more of your private life than you're comfortable giving."

"They said I wouldn't have to do trends," Mira murmured.

Delilah nodded. "They said a lot of good things. And they might mean them. But once money gets involved, people start thinking they own parts of you."

Mira swallowed. "I don't want to lose my peace."

Delilah's voice softened. "Peace is expensive," she said. "But not in dollars."

They sat with that.

Mira looked down at her hands. "Sometimes I think I'm not built for all that," she admitted. "The constant proving."

Delilah smiled slightly. "Baby, you're built for something better."

A breeze moved through the yard, the early May air smelling faintly of grass and warm soil.

"What if saying yes changes everything?" Mira asked.

Delilah answered slowly. "It will. The question is whether it changes *you*."

Later that night, the house settled into its familiar hush.

The dishes were stacked and drying. Delilah had turned off the living room lamp, leaving only the soft glow from the hallway nightlight. Outside, the air had cooled just enough to invite the windows open, cicadas beginning their steady, unhurried rhythm.

Mira sat at her desk.

The laptop was open, the partnership packet filling the screen. She read it again—not with excitement, not with fear—but with the same careful attention she gave soil before planting. She noticed the phrasing.

The assumptions. The places where flexibility was promised but not defined.

The offer was clean. Thoughtful. Reasonable.

Which meant it required discernment, not reaction.

She thought about cooking—about Salisbury steak and mashed potatoes, about green beans seasoned with ham because that was how her grandmother had taught Delilah, and Delilah had taught her. Cooking wasn't something she had picked up to be impressive. It was something she had inherited. A way of saying *I see you. You're fed here. You matter.*

Turning that into content didn't feel wrong.

Turning it into obligation did.

Mira closed the laptop and moved to her bed, sitting cross-legged against the headboard. The ceiling fan turned lazily overhead, steady and unconcerned. The room felt like it always had—safe, known, hers.

The thought arrived quietly, without drama:

If I say yes too quickly, I teach the world how to rush me.

Another followed, just as steady:

If I say yes before I understand the cost, I teach the world that my peace is negotiable.

She wasn't afraid of losing the offer.

She was afraid of losing herself inside it.

Two days later, she no longer needed to think about it.

Jaya mentioned it at lunch, casually, like gossip that didn't require guarding.

"A girl in the grade ahead of us got this cookware partnership," she said, peeling an orange. "Everyone's acting like she made it."

Mira felt her chest stay calm.

"What does she have to do?" she asked.

Jaya shrugged. "Post constantly. Film everything. They already asked her to redo a video because she didn't smile enough. She was excited at first."

She hesitated. "She doesn't sound excited anymore."

Something settled into place.

The offer hadn't been rare.

It had been timely.

And timing, Mira realized, was not the same as calling.

Mira tells Jaya, "That tracks. My mom said once money gets involved, people start thinking they own parts of you."

That afternoon, she walked through the garden alone. The plants were thriving, unbothered by comparison. Growth was happening because it was supported—not because it was being watched.

She thought about what Delilah had taught her without ever naming it:

That the right opportunities don't ask you to abandon yourself to earn them.

That losing an offer is sometimes confirmation, not failure.

That integrity compounds quietly, the way interest does.

That night, Mira sent a short, gracious reply to the brand.

She thanked them.

She declined—for now.

She did not explain herself.

She did not apologize.

She closed her laptop and lay back on her bed, the fan overhead moving in its familiar rhythm. The room felt unchanged, and yet something inside her had settled into place. There was no regret waiting for her, no second-guessing—only alignment. She knew she would meet what followed whole—unhurried, undistracted, rooted enough to wait and steady enough to grow when the season called for it.

CHAPTER FOURTEEN

The Girl Who Said Yes

Every yes carries a future inside it.

Summer arrived without asking permission.

School let out in a blur of lockers slammed shut, papers stuffed into backpacks, and promises of freedom shouted down hallways already half-forgotten. By the second week of June, the rhythm of town life had shifted—later mornings, slower afternoons, heat settling into bones and sidewalks alike.

Mira felt the difference immediately.

Her days opened up in ways they never had before. Mornings at the community garden stretched longer. Afternoons were filled with cooking, volunteering, and tending the quiet systems she loved—watering schedules, harvest rotations, lists of who needed what and when.

It was during one of those ordinary afternoons that she heard the news.

The heat had settled into the day in a way that slowed everything down. Mira stood at the long table in the shade of the garden shed, sorting green beans into neat piles—some for the assisted living center, some for Ms. Dollard, some for the cooler Delilah would load later. Her hands worked from muscle memory, snapping ends, brushing away dirt, listening to cicadas argue somewhere beyond the fence.

Her phone rang.

"Hey you," Jaya said when Mira answered, her voice bright and familiar. "I just wanted to check in before my mom drags me into another planning meeting."

Mira smiled, balancing the phone against her shoulder as she kept working. "Planning what this time?"

"Our entire summer," Jaya laughed. "We leave in two weeks. My dad's already packed—like, emotionally packed."

They fell into easy chatter, the kind that didn't rush toward anything important. Jaya talked about the mall and wanting to go one last time before she left, about finally getting waterfall braids the next morning and hoping they turned out the way she imagined. She complained—half joking, half sincere—about missing Mira's August birthday because of the trip, calling it tragic in the way only a best friend could.

"Have you even seen anyone from school lately?" Jaya asked after a pause. "Everything feels… weirdly calm. Like the quiet before something."

Mira glanced across the garden beds. "I've been seeing Eli," she said. "He's been fixing irrigation lines. Just shows up, repairs things, leaves again."

"Of course he does," Jaya said fondly.

"And I've run into Alina at the library twice already," Mira added. "We finally decided to meet on purpose next time."

"That tracks," Jaya said. "Accidental friendships only last so long."

They laughed together, the sound settling comfortably between them. Then Jaya inhaled, as if remembering something she'd meant to mention earlier.

"Oh—right," she said. "I almost forgot. The cookware deal girl from school? She signed. She's everywhere now."

Mira's fingers slowed over the basket of beans, though her hands didn't stop completely.

"Oh," she said. Not surprised. Just aware.

"She's posting constantly," Jaya continued. "Unboxings, cooking reels, sponsored captions. She already has a discount code—like, use-my-name-atcheckout kind of thing. Everyone's sharing it like it's a collective win."

Mira could picture it easily: the lighting, the angles, the urgency dressed up as gratitude.

"She sounds happy," Jaya said, then hesitated. "I mean… it's kind of a dream, right? An opportunity like that while you're still in high school."

Mira didn't argue. She didn't explain. She looked down at the beans in front of her—green, ordinary, generous.

"Yeah," she said quietly. "I'm glad for her."

They said their goodbyes, promising to talk again soon. Mira ended the call, slid her phone back into her pocket, and returned to her work.

The garden hadn't changed while she was listening.

It kept offering what it had always offered—growth without urgency, abundance without performance.

Mira snapped the next green bean and kept going.

She finished sorting the beans, washed her hands, and moved on with her day.

By early July, the posts were everywhere.

The girl's name appeared so often it became impossible not to know it. It floated through comment sections, group chats, and school threads like a brand rather than a person. She was cooking constantly now—always on camera, always smiling, always framed by clean counters and bright light. Each video looked more polished than the last, each caption more enthusiastic, more grateful, more urgent.

At first, people were thrilled.

Kids from school flooded the comments with fire emojis and exaggerated praise. Parents shared the clips proudly, tagging one another as if proximity alone granted legitimacy. Teachers liked posts quietly. Strangers asked questions that sounded supportive but weren't: *How do you do it all? What's your secret? Can you drop the routine?*

Then the tone shifted.

Someone accused her of using prechopped vegetables. Another pointed out that her onions were already translucent when the camera turned on. A comment with hundreds of likes asked whether the meal had been cooked "for real" or just styled.

The praise sharpened into scrutiny.

The audience wanted proof now. More access. More transparency. More effort.

"She has to show everything," Jaya texted one afternoon. "If she doesn't, people get mad. Like she owes them authenticity on demand."

The girl tried to keep up.

She filmed longer clips. Added disclaimers. Showed messier angles. Posted late into the night to catch different time zones. Her captions stretched, filled with explanations that sounded defensive even when they weren't meant to be.

The joy thinned anyway.

Her smiles grew sharper, like they had been practiced instead of felt. The comments grew louder and more particular—requests disguised as suggestions, entitlement disguised as feedback. The content grew repetitive, boxed in by what performed best rather than what felt true.

Jaya sent screenshots sometimes, not to gossip, but because the pattern was impossible to ignore.

"They made her redo this one three times," she said once. "The brand said the engagement dipped."

Another time: "She had to skip her cousin's birthday to film. People were asking why she wasn't posting."

Later still: "She posted at midnight. Then again at six a.m. Someone commented that she 'owed' them consistency."

Mira listened. She absorbed. She did not gloat.

She noticed how quickly excitement turned into expectation. How easily admiration became consumption. How a single yes multiplied into endless demands.

Her own summer unfolded differently.

She woke with the sun most days, the house still quiet, Delilah's coffee not yet poured. She pulled on shorts and an old T-shirt and went straight to the garden barefoot, the soil already warm beneath her feet, holding the heat of yesterday. Mornings were for checking what had changed overnight—tomatoes ripening faster than expected, zucchini swelling to impossible sizes if she turned her back for even a day, basil flowering with a generosity that felt almost excessive.

She harvested steadily, not in a rush, moving produce from plant to basket with the same care she gave people. Some of it went straight to the assisted living center. Some went to Ms. Dollard. Some ended up spread across Delilah's kitchen counters, destined to be cooked, shared, or frozen for later. Nothing felt wasted. Nothing felt forced.

One week, the neighbors asked if she could dog-sit while they were out of town. A puppy—still all paws and curiosity—took over the house for two joyful, chaotic weeks. Mira laughed more than usual, cleaning muddy footprints, redirecting chewed shoelaces, timing garden visits around naps and walks. She loved it instantly, even when it was exhausting. She knew, without needing to say it aloud, that there was no version of that summer where she could have done this while filming content on a deadline. The cat alone was already enough choreography in the kitchen.

She cooked what was abundant. Zucchini bread wrapped in foil and given away still warm. Tomato sandwiches eaten over the sink. Green beans snapped and simmered for whoever showed up hungry. When there was extra, she gave it away without thinking. When there wasn't, she adjusted.

Some afternoons, she forgot her phone entirely—left it charging on her desk while she weeded, read library books with Alina, or lay in the grass throwing sticks for the puppy. When she remembered it hours later, nothing felt missing.

Her life was full.

Not curated.

Full.

By the end of July, the shift was no longer subtle.

The girl still posted, but something brittle had crept into the edges of her videos. The smile arrived late, left early. The captions stretched longer, threaded with gratitude that sounded rehearsed rather than felt. Where there had once been ease, there was now precision—every movement calibrated, every sentence weighed for performance.

The breaking moment came quietly.

It wasn't a scandal or a dramatic announcement. It was a live video that ended too soon.

She had gone on camera to demonstrate a new pan—one the brand was pushing hard before the back-to-school season. Halfway through the recipe, her phone buzzed. A comment flashed across the screen, then another.

Why are you using boxed broth?

Didn't you say last week you make everything from scratch?

This feels lazy.

She tried to laugh it off. Adjusted the angle. Kept stirring. But the comments kept coming, stacking faster than she could read them.

You're slipping.

This isn't the quality we expect.

If you don't care anymore, just say that.

Her voice wavered when she answered. The spoon clinked too loudly against the pan. At some point, she stopped responding altogether. The screen went dark without a sign-off.

The clip was reposted everywhere.

People dissected it frame by frame. Some defended her. Others piled on, disappointed not because she had failed, but because she had stopped delivering the version of herself they felt entitled to consume.

The brand issued a polite statement later that week—supportive, distant, carefully worded. Engagement numbers dipped. Expectations didn't.

"She cried in the bathroom at the mall," Jaya said one evening, voice low. "They had her doing an in-store demo. Someone from school saw her. She was still wearing the apron."

Mira felt the weight of that settle in her chest.

The contract didn't pause for fatigue. Deadlines didn't soften for vulnerability. The audience didn't make room for being human.

"She doesn't even cook for fun anymore," Jaya added. "It's all content now. She said she misses just… making dinner."

Mira thought about her own kitchen—the way cooking still felt like refuge, like care passed hand to hand, not proof offered up for approval.

She felt no triumph.

Only relief.

She had said no to a life where joy came with a quota.

Mira turned fifteen in early August.

She thought about a party, briefly—the kind with balloons and a cake and people singing too loudly—but the idea passed as quickly as it came. What she wanted instead was quieter. Fuller. Something that felt like continuity rather than celebration.

So she packed baskets.

Banana bread first—two loaves, baked that morning, the kitchen still smelling faintly of vanilla and butter. Popsicles came next, wrapped carefully in towels and tucked into a cooler so they would survive the drive. Then produce from the garden: tomatoes still warm from the sun, cucumbers crisp and beaded with moisture, herbs tied neatly with twine the way Delilah had taught her.

Alina met her at the gate, a canvas tote slung over her shoulder. Inside it were crocheted dishcloths and lap blankets—soft cotton in pale blues and greens, stitches even and intentional. Alina smiled shyly when Mira looked inside.

"They're for whoever needs them," Alina said.

Together, they walked to Ms. Dollard's to get a ride to the assisted living center.

The lobby smelled faintly of coffee and lemon cleaner. Faces brightened as they entered, recognition spreading before Mira could even say hello. Someone reached for the cooler. Someone else took the basket of bread. Chairs were rearranged without discussion.

Mira sliced banana bread at the long table, the knife moving easily through the soft center. Alina draped blankets over knees, careful to tuck the corners just right. Popsicles were unwrapped and passed around, laughter rising as cold sweetness dripped down wrists.

Stories emerged the way they always did—unprompted and overlapping. Memories of birthdays long past. Summers that had felt endless. Small regrets softened by time.

"This," one woman said, pressing Mira's hand between both of hers, "this is the good stuff."

Mira believed her.

This was her harvest—not applause, not visibility, but presence. The kind that fed people in ways that didn't need documenting.

Late August settled gently.

Evenings cooled just enough to invite the porch. Cicadas hummed in steady rhythm as the sky deepened from blue to violet. Mira sat beside Delilah, knees drawn up, a glass of iced tea sweating slowly on the railing.

"I'm glad I didn't say yes," Mira said finally.

Delilah didn't look surprised. She had been waiting for the sentence.

"I know," she replied.

Mira traced a faint crack in the porch wood with her finger. "I don't think I would've survived it."

Delilah smiled, not unkindly. "You would've survived," she said. "You're strong. But survival isn't the same as wholeness."

Mira considered that.

"Some opportunities ask you to trade pieces of yourself," Delilah continued. "They don't take them all at once. Just a little at a time. By the time you notice, you're negotiating for things you used to give freely."

Mira leaned her head against Delilah's shoulder, the weight of the summer settling into something like certainty.

Across town, contracts continued to tick forward. Metrics refreshed. Expectations recalibrated.

Here, the season closed without ceremony. No announcements marked its ending, no photographs sealed it into memory. The garden simply slowed, the evenings softened, and the house settled back into its familiar rhythms. Mira did not feel as though she had missed something that others had found. She felt as though she had been paying attention all along. The summer had not rushed her or tested her worth; it had strengthened it quietly. What she carried forward was not regret or longing, but readiness—a steadiness rooted in knowing who she was, what she valued, and how to wait without fear. She wasn't behind. She was aligned, grounded, and exactly where she needed to be.

CHAPTER FIFTEEN

Without Announcement

Not all attention arrives with a spotlight. Some of it comes quietly, to see what holds when no one is watching.

They went to the store with a list and a loose sense of time.

Delilah pushed the cart slowly, the way she always did, reading the aisle signs out of habit rather than need. Eggs. Milk. Juice. Rice. Potatoes. Tea bags. And—if they were still warm—butter croissants from the bakery, because Mira loved them and Delilah believed in small mercies.

The automatic doors slid open and the smell hit them immediately: sugar and yeast, cinnamon and heat. The bakery case glowed under soft lights, trays of pastries lined up like promises.

"Just one treat," Delilah said, already reaching for a bin.

"Sugar cookies," Mira said, smiling.

They added them to the cart and moved on.

To save time, Delilah sent Mira ahead for the milk and eggs while she doubled back toward dry goods.

Mira crossed the store, past end caps stacked with summer promotions, the hum of refrigeration growing louder as she reached the cool air of the dairy section.

That was when she noticed the woman.

At first, it was nothing more than proximity. The woman was in the same aisle, moving at a similar pace. Mid-forties, maybe. Practical shoes. Canvas tote instead of a purse. Mira grabbed the eggs, then hesitated, deciding to take a different route back—cutting through frozen foods instead of looping past produce.

The woman changed direction too.

Not immediately. Not obviously. Just enough to register.

Mira paused at the freezer doors, pretending to scan labels. The woman stopped a few feet away, reading the back of a bag of peas with deliberate focus. Mira felt no fear. No alarm. Just awareness—like realizing someone is walking at the same rhythm as you without meaning to.

She took the milk and headed toward the center of the store, where tea and rice were shelved. As she turned into the aisle, the woman slowed, as if considering whether she needed something there. She didn't follow. She didn't stop Mira.

Mira found Delilah comparing olive oil prices, turning one bottle slightly to read the label.

It was then that the feeling returned—not stared down, not chased. Simply noticed.

The woman stood a few feet away near the produce scales. She weighed tomatoes slowly, deliberately, as if she wasn't in a hurry to be anywhere else.

When their eyes met, the woman smiled.

Not the smile of recognition. Not excitement. Just acknowledgment.

Then she turned back to her tomatoes.

Mira added the milk and eggs to the cart. Delilah glanced up.

"Everything okay?" she asked.

"Yeah," Mira said truthfully.

They finished shopping. Paid. Walked out into the heat.

As Delilah loaded the groceries into the trunk, Mira looked back through the glass doors. The woman was still inside, now speaking quietly to the cashier, tote resting at her feet.

Mira didn't feel watched in a way that demanded action.

She felt… observed.

She held the thought loosely, the way she held most things—without panic, without dismissal.

Some awareness, she had learned, did not need interpretation right away.

Remembering her promise to stop by and help, Mira told Delilah—and Professor Butterbean—that she would be back within the hour. The cat lifted one disinterested eye from the windowsill. Delilah nodded, already rinsing a cutting board.

Mira stepped outside, repositioned a flowerpot that had tilted sideways in the heat, and jogged down the sidewalk toward Ms. Dollard's house. Cicadas rattled in the trees, the air thick with late-afternoon warmth and the smell of cut grass. She slowed only when she reached the porch, breath steady, hair sticking slightly to the back of her neck.

Ms. Dollard opened the door before Mira knocked.

"There you are," she said warmly. "Right on time—or close enough that it counts."

Inside, the house smelled faintly of paper and lemon polish. Sunlight filtered through sheer curtains, settling softly on shelves that always seemed to need just a bit of tending.

"Can I get you something to drink?" Ms. Dollard asked.

"I'm okay," Mira replied. "Just came to help."

They exchanged the usual pleasantries as they gathered the books—how the day had gone, how the heat was behaving, how grateful Ms. Dollard felt to still wake up able to move through her own rooms.

"It's a blessing," she said, stacking a small pile carefully. "Being in the land of the living another day. No need to rush growing old when there's still so much to notice."

They worked quietly for a moment, the soft thump of books finding their places the only sound.

Then Ms. Dollard glanced over. "And how has your day been so far, Mira?"

Mira hesitated, then smiled slightly. "Pretty normal," she said. "Except… something odd happened at the grocery store."

She told the story carefully—not dramatically. The woman. The way their paths seemed to mirror each other. The awareness without fear.

"I don't know if she was actually following me," Mira said, sliding a book into place. "It just felt… deliberate."

Ms. Dollard listened without interruption, her

expression thoughtful rather than alarmed.

"That's interesting," she said at last. "Because someone asked me about you recently."

Mira's hand stilled on the shelf.

"About the garden," Ms. Dollard continued. "How long it's been running. Who keeps it organized. She wasn't intrusive. Just… observant."

She described the woman plainly. Practical shoes. Canvas tote. Calm eyes.

Mira felt the recognition settle.

"That's her," she said quietly.

Ms. Dollard nodded once. "I thought it might be."

Mira searched her face. "That doesn't worry you?"

Ms. Dollard smiled gently. "No. People who ask questions like that aren't usually looking for something to take. They're trying to understand what holds up over time."

The books stood neatly now. The room looked the same—but Mira wasn't.

The unease she might have expected never arrived. Instead, there was only the quiet awareness of being seen, without urgency or demand.

Mira told Delilah about it that evening while they worked side by side in the kitchen.

The windows were open, letting in the sound of cicadas and the faint smell of warm pavement after a late afternoon shower. Delilah washed dishes slowly, methodically, as Mira dried and set them into the cabinet. It was the kind of work that allowed space for conversation without demanding it.

"There was a woman at the store," Mira said, keeping her tone light. "I couldn't tell if she was following me or just… moving the same way I was."

Delilah didn't look up right away. "How did it feel?" she asked.

"Not bad," Mira said after a moment. "Just noticeable."

Delilah nodded, as if that distinction mattered. She set a plate on the rack and reached for the towel. "Then it's probably not something to borrow trouble over," she said. "Sometimes people notice us for reasons we don't understand yet."

Mira leaned against the counter. "Ms. Dollard said someone asked her about the garden. Same woman, I think."

That made Delilah pause.

She rested her hands on the counter, thinking. "I don't know what that means," she said honestly. "And I don't need to."

Mira looked at her.

"There was a time in my life when I thought I had to understand everything immediately," Delilah continued. "Name it. Control it. Prepare for it. That never actually made me safer. It just made me tired."

She smiled faintly. "What kept me steady was learning to trust how things felt instead of racing to explain them."

"So you're not worried?" Mira asked.

"I'm attentive," Delilah said. "There's a difference."

They finished the dishes in companionable quiet. Delilah turned off the sink and wiped her hands dry.

"If someone is paying attention to you," she said carefully, "it doesn't automatically mean they want something from you. And if they do, you'll know when it's time to decide what to do about it."

Delilah's words stayed with her as she slid the last glass into the cabinet. Attention, she realized, wasn't the same as threat. It didn't require response. It didn't ask her to shrink or perform.

She rested her palms briefly on the counter, steady and present, and let that truth settle.

"Whatever it is," Delilah added, softer now, "we don't change who we are just because someone's looking."

Mira nodded. That part, at least, felt certain.

Nothing followed immediately.

No phone call. No email. No neatly packaged explanation that would make sense of the grocery store or the quiet questions Ms. Dollard had responded to at the library. The woman did not reappear in any obvious way. No one asked Mira to sit down and tell her story. No one asked for permission to observe.

Life continued, which Mira had come to understand was often how meaningful things revealed themselves. At school, the noise around influence culture had dulled into something heavier. The cookware girl still attended classes, but the shine had worn thin. She missed assignments. Asked for extensions. Whispered conversations followed her down the hallways—not admiration now, but curiosity edged with judgment. By mid-fall, the story finally surfaced: she had parted ways with the cookware company.

The contract, it turned out, had come with an advance—thirty thousand dollars paid upfront against projected sales. The agreement was standard:

the advance would be earned back gradually through commissions as products sold. But sales had barely moved. When she pulled out early, overwhelmed and unable to keep up with the demands, the balance didn't disappear. It converted to a repayment obligation, spread over time but very real.

The number traveled quickly. Thirty thousand dollars.

Teachers stopped speculating. Students stopped envying. Parents went quiet. The situation was no longer aspirational—it was cautionary. The girl stopped posting altogether. Her account remained online like a storefront with the lights off.

Mira noticed all of this from a distance. She felt no relief that it hadn't been her. Only certainty. The path she hadn't taken had teeth.

The garden needed closing out. Beds were cleared and amended. Tools were cleaned and returned to their hooks. At the assisted living center, the rhythm of volunteering stayed the same—meals prepared, stories shared, laughter exchanged without announcement.

What Mira did not know—what she could not have known—was that the questions had never been about gathering information.

They were about listening.

When someone asked Ms. Dollard how long the garden had been running, they already knew the answer. What they wanted was to hear how Ms. Dollard spoke about Mira when no one was recording, no one was scoring points, and there was nothing to gain from exaggeration.

When a volunteer coordinator asked who decided what to cook each week, it wasn't to check credentials. It was to see whether the answer came wrapped in ego or offered freely, with credit shared easily.

These questions were invitations, not tests.

They allowed space for truth to surface naturally—unguarded, unpolished, sincere.

Mira felt none of this directly. She simply noticed that people spoke her name with steadiness. Not awe. Not envy. Familiar respect.

She continued doing the work the same way she always had.

By the time winter edged closer, the world had moved on to something else—as it always did.

At school, attention shifted to exams, college tours, holiday performances. The cookware story faded into rumor, then into silence. The girl's name stopped appearing in conversations altogether, replaced by whatever new spectacle had arrived to take its place.

Mira did not track any of it closely.

Her days filled themselves.

The garden beds rested under mulch now, earth tucked in against the cold. The pantry shelves held jars from earlier months—tomatoes, beans, herbs—small proofs of a season that had already given what it could. At the assisted living center, the menu changed with the weather. Soups replaced salads. Banana bread gave way to loaves studded with walnuts and cranberries.

Thanksgiving came quietly.

Mira spent the morning helping Delilah in the kitchen, chopping onions, peeling potatoes, listening to stories she had heard before and loved anyway. Later, she packed containers for the elders who couldn't travel, for Ms. Dollard, for anyone who would receive them without needing explanation.

Nothing about it felt like achievement.

It felt like continuity.

Outside, the world kept chasing visibility, mistaking noise for momentum. Inside Mira's life, things remained grounded, unremarkable in the way sturdy things often are.

If something was forming beyond her view, it did not announce itself.

And Mira did not need it to.

Her life was already full.

CHAPTER SIXTEEN

Legacy Has a Voice

What you inherit is not always named. Sometimes it lives in the way you move through the world.

Mira had stopped by that morning just before noon, the hour when the light softened and the house felt most awake. She brought croissants from the bakery—still faintly warm, wrapped carefully in paper—and a small tin of tea Ms. Dollard liked but never remembered to buy for herself.

She had noticed, over the past year, how Ms. Dollard moved more slowly now. How the pauses between standing and sitting had grown longer. How the quiet in the house had deepened. Mira responded the way she always did to things that mattered: by showing up.

Her visits had become intentional. Regular enough to be counted on. Not announced, not grand—just steady. A reason for Ms. Dollard to expect company. To know that someone would come.

Her children hadn't visited that past Christmas. They'd called, sent cards, promised a spring trip that never materialized. Mira never asked about it directly, but she saw the way Ms. Dollard lingered a little longer at the assisted living center during the holiday drive, how she folded herself into the room full of laughter and warmth as if claiming it.

That day, they sat at the small table near the window, steam rising from their cups, crumbs scattering lightly across the placemat.

Ms. Dollard asked Mira how things had been going with the dog that lived next door. Mira smiled as she told her about the Parkers and their golden retriever, about how the dog had taken to her immediately, following her from room to room, curling at her feet while she read or cooked. She mentioned that she'd been pet sitting more often lately, earning a little money here and there, but mostly enjoying the simple rhythm of it.

"I don't feel stressed about it at all," Mira said, brushing crumbs from the table. "It's not a burden. I like helping them. It just fits."

Ms. Dollard listened, nodding slowly, her expression thoughtful.

"That's usually how it goes," she replied. "The things that matter most don't announce themselves while they're happening. They make sense later, when you're finally quiet enough to see the shape they made."

She smiled as she said it, the kind of smile that held memory inside it, then set her teacup down as if she had been waiting for the right moment to speak.

"I still can't get over how well the Christmas Give Back Drive turned out," she said. "I don't think I've ever seen anything quite like it—certainly not organized by three teenagers who were supposedly just 'helping out.'"

Mira laughed softly, but her mind had already slipped back to the weeks leading up to it.

It had started simply. Flyers sketched out at the kitchen table, markers bleeding through cheap paper. Mira, Jaya, and Alina debating wording—how to ask without sounding desperate, how to invite without pressure. In the end, the flyers were plain and honest: *Winter Give Back Drive. Gently used clothing. New toys. Shoes. Gift cards. Non-perishable food. Anything helps.*

They taped them everywhere.

School hallways. Bulletin boards at the grocery store. The library entrance. A corkboard near the café that smelled perpetually of burnt coffee and cinnamon. Mira hadn't expected much. None of them had.

Then the donations started coming.

Bags of folded coats still smelling faintly of laundry soap. Boxes of brand-new sneakers with tags intact. Plush toys tucked into clean plastic bins, their fur brushed smooth. Gift cards slipped quietly into envelopes. Cash donations handed over with murmured blessings and embarrassed smiles.

By the end of the second week, the assisted living center's community room was full.

Tables lined the walls, neatly arranged piles sorted by size and season. The sound of laughter echoed off the linoleum floors as volunteers moved back and forth, carrying boxes, straightening stacks, greeting families as they arrived. The air smelled like roasted chicken, garlic, and herbs—Delilah and Mira had been cooking since early morning, moving around each other with practiced ease.

In the kitchen, pots simmered gently. Steam fogged the windows. Mira stirred gravy while Delilah checked trays of vegetables, the warmth of the room wrapping around them like reassurance.

Ms. Dollard had led the prayer before the doors opened, her voice steady and unadorned, asking simply for warmth, dignity, and enough for everyone.

Thirty-two families came through that afternoon.

Some arrived hesitant, eyes downcast. Others brought children who darted ahead, drawn by the promise of color and noise. Shoes were tried on. Coats were zipped. Stuffed animals found their way into small arms. Thank-yous were spoken quietly, sometimes through tears, sometimes through laughter that felt like relief.

Alina sat at one of the tables crocheting hats as fast as her fingers would allow, smiling each time someone paused to watch. Jaya moved through the room with a clipboard, then abandoned it entirely, choosing instead to sit on the floor with a little girl who refused to let go of a purple bear.

When it was over, the room looked ordinary again.

But it felt different.

"There was so much joy," Ms. Dollard said now, her voice softer. "So much gratitude. And not a single moment of spectacle."

Mira nodded. She remembered how someone had taken a few photos, how a short video clip had been posted later. It hadn't gone viral. There were no trending hashtags, no surge of attention.

Too quiet, perhaps.

But the warmth had lingered long after the room was cleaned and the last family had gone home.

Ms. Dollard looked at Mira with something like reverence. "You brought people together," she said. "That's not something you can manufacture."

Mira felt the truth of it settle gently, the way good things often did in her life—without noise, without needing proof.

Ms. Dollard rose slowly from her chair and moved

toward the small desk by the window, the one she used more often now than the larger writing table she'd retired years earlier. Papers were stacked neatly, not in piles but in thoughtful groupings, each held together with intention rather than haste.

"You know," she said, adjusting a folder, "people always misunderstand what an archivist does."

Mira watched her, attentive.

"They think it's about preserving the impressive things," Ms. Dollard continued. "The official records. The moments someone already decided were important." She smiled faintly. "But the real work is quieter than that."

She opened a drawer and removed a small box, worn smooth at the edges. Inside were photographs, handwritten notes, programs from long-forgotten events—ordinary things that had outlasted the noise around them.

"Archives are built from what people overlook," she said. "From daily efforts. From consistency. From lives that don't demand attention but shape everything that comes after."

Mira felt the words settle somewhere deep.

"When I was working," Ms. Dollard went on, "I learned that the most reliable stories were never the loudest ones. They were the ones that showed up the same way year after year. No performance. No revision."

She met Mira's eyes then. "That's why people ask questions they already know the answers to. They aren't gathering facts. They're listening for tone. For truth. For consistency."

Mira thought of the grocery store. The library. The questions that hadn't felt invasive, only patient.

"So they're… preserving?" Mira asked.

Ms. Dollard smiled. "Not you as a person. But the pattern you're part of."

She closed the box gently and returned it to the drawer.

"Some things," she said, "are worth keeping exactly as they are."

They returned to the table, the tea long since cooled, the light outside shifting almost imperceptibly toward evening. Ms. Dollard did not seem in a hurry to say anything else. She folded her hands, then unfolded them, as if deciding how much of herself to place into words.

"When you spend your life working with records," she said at last, "you learn something most people never have to think about."

Mira waited.

"You learn how much gets lost," Ms. Dollard continued. "Not because it wasn't important, but because no one thought to keep it. Ordinary goodness disappears first. Quiet effort. Care that didn't ask to be remembered."

She gestured around the room—the shelves, the framed photos, the carefully kept objects that told a life without spectacle. "An archive isn't built to prove someone mattered. It exists because they did."

Mira felt a small tightening in her chest. Not sadness—recognition.

"I used to catalog community records," Ms. Dollard said. "Church suppers. School events. Neighborhood projects. Things people laughed about later and said didn't really count." She smiled, not unkindly. "Those were the very things that held towns together."

She looked at Mira then, directly but gently. "What you and those girls did at Christmas—that's the kind of thing that vanishes if no one pays attention. Not because it wasn't meaningful. Because it didn't shout."

Mira thought of the flyers. The folding tables. The families lingering in the doorway, unsure whether they were welcome.

"I don't think I did anything special," Mira said.

Ms. Dollard nodded. "That's exactly it."

She reached for her teacup, took a slow sip, then set it down again. "History doesn't survive on special moments alone. It survives on people who show up without asking who's watching."

There was no implication in her tone. No suggestion of hidden systems or unseen judges. Just a lifetime of observing what endured.

"I suppose," Ms. Dollard added, almost to herself, "that's why it always matters to me when someone asks about the garden, or the meals, or the way you move through your days. It tells me someone else has noticed what usually slips through the cracks."

Mira absorbed that quietly.

Outside, a car passed, tires whispering over pavement. Somewhere nearby, a door closed with a familiar click. The world continued in its ordinary way, indifferent to the conversation unfolding inside a modest living room that smelled faintly of tea and warm pastry.

Ms. Dollard watched the light shift across the floor before she spoke again. When she did, her voice carried the calm authority of someone who had lived long enough to know what endured.

"There's a saying," she said, eyes still on the window. "When there is no enemy within, the enemy without can do no harm."

Mira felt the words settle, not as instruction, but as confirmation.

"Most people spend their lives trying to control what's outside of them," Ms. Dollard continued. "The noise. The opinions. The chaos. They believe peace is something the world has to give them." She turned back to Mira then, gentle but precise. "It isn't."

She folded her hands together. "Peace is something you cultivate. Quietly. Internally. And once you do, the world loses its power to knock you off center."

Mira thought of her classmates—how quickly they flared, how easily they were shaken by praise or slight, how desperately they chased affirmation that never seemed to last. She thought of trends that burned hot and disappeared, of outrage that fed on itself.

"That's what so many young people don't understand right now," Ms. Dollard said, as if reading the thought. "They're trying to manage the storm instead of strengthening the house."

Mira smiled faintly. "My mom always says you can't

build a life around reacting."

Ms. Dollard nodded. "Your mother learned that the hard way."

The statement carried no drama. Just truth.

"She went through fire," Ms. Dollard went on, "so you wouldn't have to. That's how inheritance works when it's done right. Not money. Not opportunity. But clarity."

Mira felt a warmth spread through her chest—pride, gratitude, something like awe.

"That's why you're different," Ms. Dollard said. "Not because you're louder. Not because you're exceptional in the ways people usually mean. But because you are not at war with yourself."

She let that sit.

"You may never be famous," Ms. Dollard added, a trace of humor in her voice. "You may never trend or be chased by cameras. But you are rich in something far more durable."

Mira looked down at her hands, at the faint calluses from garden tools, the ink stains from flyers, the small scars that told quiet stories.

"Moral wealth," Ms. Dollard said. "Ethical currency. The kind that compounds over time."

The room felt full—not crowded, but complete.

Mira nodded, the understanding settling not as pressure or expectation, but as grounding. She had never wanted to be extraordinary in the ways the world applauded.

She had only ever wanted to be whole.

And as she sat there, listening to the soft sounds of a life well lived around her, she understood that this—this quiet alignment, this internal steadiness—was not an ending.

It was a doorway.

www.ingramcontent.com/pod-product-compliance
Lightning Source LLC
LaVergne TN
LVHW091133080826
845145LV00008B/2131